BETTER
WATCH
OUT

BETTER WATCH OUT

jim krochka

DEDICATED TO JAYMEE

CHAPTERS

Foreword   i

Preface   v

Chapter 1 – CHRISTMAS DAY   1

Chapter 2 – TWO WEEKS EARLIER   5

Chapter 3 – BACK TO CHRISTMAS DAY   15

Chapter 4 – CAN RALPH COOPERATE?   29

Chapter 5 – MY CYBER BABY   35

Chapter 6 – TAKE ME TO BELIZE   53

Chapter 7 – BACK HOME AGAIN   61

Chapter 8 – FRED GETS SERIOUS
            (OR MORE SERIOUS)   69

Chapter 9 – A SYMBIOTIC RELATIONSHIP?   81

Chapter 10 – TIME TO TRAIN   99

Chapter 11 – THE BIG PUSH   121

Chapter 12 – THE RACE IS ON   147

Chapter 13 – HALF MARATHON DAY   187

Chapter 14 – WEDDING DAY   191

Chapter 15 – GOIN' TO MONTANA   195

Chapter 16 – CONVERSATIONS WITH FRED   213

FOREWORD

Have you ever had a computer hallucinate while working on it? I have!

I'm a comparative psychologist, and one evening, while working on a talk about the natural history of vision, I asked a well-known AI system for a summary of how vision evolved. Almost instantly, it printed out a very readable and seemingly credible summary. The report even included quotations from the articles it referenced. Here's the only problem: The articles and their quotations don't exist!

The bottom line: If I had not verified the AI-reported references, I would have used them in my talk – to my embarrassment!

As it turns out, what happened to me is not an isolated problem. AI developers are not only aware that their programs will create imaginary research reports, but they also have a name for it:

AI hallucinations! Even now, developers are trying to understand why their programs create imaginary research documents.

After a recent bike ride, during which Jim and I talked about my AI experience, Jim asked if I would read a draft of his book *Better Watch Out*. I did, and I found an engaging, funny story about how a family bought their father an AI-based watch called Fred to be his personal trainer and help him improve his health. Fred would monitor Ralph's habits and make suggestions for his diet and physical training routines.

With that introduction, if you think this will be another self-improvement book and are ready to set the book down – don't! What you're going to find is a light-hearted love story – a romantic comedy. Ralph, a widower, meets a wonderful woman, Annie. But programming missteps by Fred, the AI watch, threaten the budding relationship between Ralph and Annie – like when it learns how to punish Ralph with electrical shocks when he overeats.

As the story unfolds, Ralph and Annie learn about the shortcomings of an AI watch, and Fred learns how best to deal with humans! How that comes about makes this romantic comedy a joy to read.

A note to AI fans: An interesting element of the story, Fred, the AI watch, becomes frustrated with his inability to motivate Ralph to improve his health. Fred engages the help of a "female" AI watch called Sam. Their collaborative search for ways to help Ralph runs into the ethical and moral issues that might face AI developers today. Should Fred always tell Ralph the truth? Should Fred, without its developers' knowledge, obtain the capabilities not programmed by humans?

But perhaps most fascinating, *Better Watch Out* raises the interesting question of whether an AI system and humans can become friends!

Tom Bennett
University of Michigan, BA
Michigan State University, MA, PhD

PREFACE

Who am I, and where did the idea for this book come from? My name is James (Jim) Krochka. Some things about me – I am an attorney (semi-retired), I have been a Certified Public Accountant, and I was a consultant in the Silicon Valley during the Dot-Com Bubble – from the people side, not the high-tech side. That is why this book is focused on the interaction between people and high-tech, not the tech part. I live in Walnut Creek, CA, and am married to Brenda. I have a daughter – Jaymee, and two stepdaughters – Amanda and Lindsey.

I have done creative things before. I have over 20 songs on iTunes and other music sources. Some of the songs are indirectly referenced in *Better Watch Out* – "My Cyber Baby," "Goin' To Montana," and "Take Me To Belize." I wrote the music and lyrics for all the songs and performed them along with some much better musicians than me. Other songs of interest – are "Amelia, We Need You" (for people like me who think the world needs someone as brave, decent, and intelligent as Amelia Earhart), "Want The Short Line" (A rock song about hating to wait in line for stuff), "Sleep Like A Cat" (a rap song for kids and adults that have seen cats sleep and wish they could sleep as deeply as a cat – we have 12 cats so I've seen a few sleeping), "Fury At The Wall" (a song about a Civil War battle at Gettysburg), "Where Have The Leaders Gone?" (for those of us who wonder about whether our political system is becoming dysfunctional.) There are others as well.

Also, charity work is important – I served on the board of directors of Meals On Wheels and the board of directors of Senior Legal Services for years until my terms were up. I look forward to hopefully being a docent at the Oakland Zoo. I recently joined the board of the local Kiwanis Club.

So, what is *Better Watch Out* about? It is fictional, but it could happen. After all, will a watch be able to control our lives more and more? I think absolutely. The idea for this book came from an actual event. I was in Sunriver, Oregon – near Bend – and Brenda was home in Walnut Creek, CA. We typically text in the morning when we wake up apart. She was still in bed, and I was up. I said I felt like staying in bed. She said, "You should," and I said that my watch made me get up. She, of course, said to ignore it. I said it kept shocking me until I got out of bed (and started laughing). Then, I thought, that will be a watch feature someday. The idea for running a 10k came from my daughter, Jaymee. We ran in the Walnut Creek Turkey Trot. My legs never hurt so badly, even though I do lots of athletic activities, so I thought I was in good shape.

Well, there you have it. It didn't dawn on me immediately to write a book because I never had done so, but the thought wouldn't let go. I kept thinking of situations where the watch could be annoying, helpful, interesting, fun, encouraging, etc. I am not an engineer or computer scientist, but I have been around some high-tech people who went on to create multi-billion-dollar companies, and many more that failed. Some of it was luck – good or bad – some of it was skill. Usually both. This book is about the reaction of people, in particular Ralph, to high-tech. Ralph is not a high-tech expert. In fact, he doesn't really like high-tech gadgets – kind of like me and many of my friends. But it is sometime in the future, and his daughter Joanie buys him the latest smartwatch for Christmas.

To some extent, *Better Watch Out* explores what artificial intelligence is capable of, but I (the author) am not an AI technical expert, so a reader should look elsewhere for algorithms, etc. This is a people book.

Jim Krochka

This is not a Christmas story. However, it does involve a Christmas gift, but those are usually fun when you get them and still appreciated months later. Thus, this is not a Christmas story because, as time went by, the gift became a nightmare and a joy. High-tech gifts can be like that.

Chapter 1

CHRISTMAS DAY

It was a wonderful day. The Holden family was gathered at the home of Ralph Holden – the 57-year-old father of 2 adult children – Joanie and William, and their children. It was so nice to have everyone together this Christmas because Joanie and William had moved away and had to join Christmas celebrations via a video call for the last two years. Ralph's wife Jane (Joanie and William's mother) had passed away suddenly five years ago. Ralph was still recovering from that awful day.

Since it was still morning, the grandchildren were busy shouting into each adult's bedroom, "IT'S CHRISTMAS!" (In an effort to assist the uninformed who might have thought Christmas was on the

26th) The result was that the adults felt the usual mixture of stress and joy that people who celebrate Christmas feel that morning. Ralph had put up an 8½ foot Christmas tree, so there was plenty of room for the numerous presents resting below and around the tree.

Time to go crazy! Joanie played Santa – identifying and handing out gifts accordingly. The usual array of high-tech gifts was given to the children – video games, cell phones, drones, VR devices, etc. As for the adults, they got the usual sweaters, running pants, gift certificates, jewelry, socks, hats, etc., etc. Most of which will never be used or seen again.

Except for Ralph. He opened a gift and saw a fairly small box that said: "UH EXTREME." Joanie yelled, "Do you like it, Dad?"

Because Ralph had not opened the box, he had no idea what it was, so all he could say was, "I don't know yet."

Joanie yelled, "Open it." as though he might not have thought of that himself.

So, Ralph did just that. Upon opening it, he learned that "UH EXTREME" stood for Ultra-Healthy Extreme – the top of the line. Ralph had told Joanie and William that he had made a fair amount of money sports betting over the internet and had saved enough to create some free time.

"I've been sitting on my butt so long – it's time for me to live a healthier lifestyle," he would say to them. Joanie and William took that information to heart and got Ralph something that could help him achieve his healthier lifestyle goal. Ralph stared at his gift.

Chapter 2

TWO WEEKS EARLIER

"What should we get Dad for Christmas?" asked Joanie.

William replied, "The usual – socks, a bottle of wine, a wallet, and tickets to a football game or maybe basketball."

Joanie thought about it and was determined to get something personal. Something that Ralph wanted and could use. Joanie recalled Ralph talking about the new healthy lifestyle he was going to have, so it made sense to give him something to help him attain that lifestyle. "How about a healthy food plan?"

William replied, "Knowing Dad, I think that food will end up spoiling in the fridge." Joanie could not help but agree. She recalled seeing food in his fridge that had expired maybe decades before. It was as though he thought the fridge was a time capsule for people 50 years later to learn about the diet of their ancestors.

"How about a set of weights?" William said.

"Are you crazy?" said Joanie immediately. "A set of weights should only be given to someone already in shape," she said. Otherwise, the first use will result in tremendous muscle pain, and the weights will be put to other uses (e.g., as a doorstop) or not at all. William agreed with her, so, again, it was back to square one.

Joanie searched the internet for health-promoting gifts. After scrolling down a few items, she saw smartwatches. Of course, Joanie and William had one (along with their kids), but Ralph did not. He was so caught up in sports betting that he had no need for one – now he did. The capabilities of watches had increased dramatically over the past few years, so it was necessary to find one that made the most sense.

AI (artificial intelligence) was all the rage, so getting up to speed was necessary before deciding. Joanie agreed to take on the task.

"So, what is AI anyway?" she thought. After some research, she concluded that a particular type of AI called Means-end analysis (MEA) was used extensively. It would find a sequence of actions that lead to a desired goal. It simply connects to the outside environment by sensory channel (sound, body functions, sights, etc.) and then determines what actions need to be taken to obtain the goal that it has been given.

The UH EXTREME was ranked as the most advanced smartwatch for those wanting to have a healthy lifestyle. It did the usual stuff like monitor heart rate, count steps, count calories, bicycle mileage, etc. But it did something more – much more. It got to know the wearer personally, really personally. When the wearer first put it on, the wearer would recite a poem so that the watch would recognize the wearer's voice. That way, the watch could know what the wearer is saying and use that information when designing a program for the wearer. Also, the watch had a camera to see what the wearer saw. Again, more information for decision-making. In addition, the watch monitored the wearer's bodily functions – even more information. The watch would use all that information to help the wearer achieve the goals set by the wearer.

Although the UH EXTREME was the latest model, there were reviews by people who participated in studies when the UH EXTREME was being designed. There were even some very recent reviews by people who had bought one. The reviews were glowing – otherwise, they would not end up in an ad. Like these:

"I lost fifty pounds and gained 20% more muscle mass in nine months," said Frederic.

"I slimmed down to a size four from a size fourteen in six months," said Jessica.

"Be like Frederic and Jessica!" said the AI Me ad. There were more reviews, but clearly, it was perfect for Ralph.

Joanie was convinced but had to see the watch

for herself. It seemed the UH EXTREME was what Ralph needed. "He can put it on and immediately start using it without any pain, risk of spoilage, etc.," she said.

She thought it was great that the watch would, in a way, become Ralph's personal friend. Since the death of their mother, Jane, five years earlier, their Dad had isolated himself too much. The UH EXTREME could be perfect for him! A friend who can guide him through daily life and help him create the healthy lifestyle he desires.

"Wow, that really does sound perfect," said William. "Something that could become intimately familiar with Dad – especially now that we all live far apart – is what Dad needs," added William.

"In addition, the UH EXTREME could share information with us - if Dad lets it - so we could stay up-to-date on how Dad is doing," said Joanie.

They normally buy online, but they decided to go to a store so they could handle it and try it out to see what it can do. The UH EXTREME was made by a company called AI Me. AI Me had its own stores where it sold various high-tech items it made and tried its best to get customers locked into subscription services through equipment manufactured and sold through AI Me. For example, if someone wanted to take a trip to Hawaii, the person could purchase headgear and then add on devices that could simulate being in Hawaii. What made it special was that, as the user used the equipment and software, AI tweaks the experience based on the user's emotional reactions. The downside was that some customers enjoyed the experience so much that they kept on the headgear for hours and hours, ignoring family, work, school, etc.

When Joanie and William walked into the store, they were greeted at the door.

"What can we help you with today?" the greeter named Wallace asked.

"Well, we're here to look at the UH EXTREME," Joanie said.

"Excellent choice," said Wallace. "We are getting lots of people in. It really is quite special. Nothing like it out there! I love mine."

"Our Dad wants to get in shape, so we thought the UH EXTREME could help him," said William.

"It will absolutely, my man. Your dad will have no choice but to get in shape once he has the UH EXTREME on his wrist."

"Perfect," said Joanie.

"Well then, head over to the right-hand corner." Wallace pointed. "You'll see the watch section. Enjoy yourselves." Joanie and William thanked Wallace and moved on.

The watch section of AI Me's store had lots of options to choose from, but clearly, the UH EXTREME was the star of the show. So many people were gathered around looking at it, asking questions, putting it on, and testing its functions that it took a while to talk to an AI Me rep.

Finally, it was their turn. "Hey guys, what can I do for you?" said Brenda.

"We're here to look at and try out the UH EXTREME," replied Joanie.

"Fantastic!! The UH EXTREME is **the** top-of-the-line in the entire world of smartwatches. Years of research went into it, and the AI makes the watch into a personal friend for life. It is especially useful for someone who wants to get into better physical condition – it pretty much takes over for the wearer. Thus, the wearer really has no choice but to follow the program," said Brenda.

"Perfect, my dad can be lazy," said William.

"That's for sure," said Joanie.

"OK, here you go," said Brenda as she pulled a sample UH EXTREME out of the case. The design was amazingly sleek – like an animal waiting to pounce. The color was black and turquoise – it reminded Joanie of snorkeling in Hawaii. There was only one knob.

"Almost all commands and correspondence are done verbally. The watch is able to talk to the wearer just like a friend. In fact, the watch listens even when the wearer is not talking to it. The more the watch knows about the wearer, the better it can design a program that meets the wearer's goals," said Brenda.

"Outstanding!" exclaimed Joanie.

"The easier it is for my dad, the better. He really shies away from complicated high-tech stuff," added William.

"Then he is exactly the customer this watch was designed for – someone in need of a device that takes control. Plus, with the wireless electric feature, the wearer does not have to take off the watch for charging. It charges while on the wrist of the wearer," said Brenda.

"Let me put it on you and show you how it works," said Brenda to Joanie. Brenda connected the clasp of the watch onto Brenda's wrist. The clasp adjusted itself to Joanie's wrist size.

"Wow, that is cool – it fits my wrist perfectly!" said Joanie.

"Yes, the UH EXTREME is incredibly comfortable because it will fit any wearer's wrist perfectly," said Brenda.

"Plus, the clasp and band seem really substantial – even though they are so light-weight," said Joanie.

"Yes, the materials were invented just for the UH EXTREME. They are practically indestructible. The goal is to ensure the watch never accidentally falls off," said Brenda.

"Makes sense. If I'm wearing this expensive watch, I don't want it falling off and breaking on the floor. But I'm not convinced Dad would actually wear it and doubt he would use it to reach his health goals," said William.

"What else can we get him? He needs this watch. I will get him to wear and use it," Joanie said.

"Plus, it's very expensive. Let's wait and think," said William.

"If Dad does not wear and use it, I will pay you your half back. Come on, let's do it. Do it for Dad," said Joanie.

"OK, but make sure you pay me back if he doesn't wear it and use it," said William.

"You're my brother, and I love you, but you are a jerk!" said Joanie

Brenda interrupted, "OK, Joanie, I want you to read this phrase out loud. First, say the watch's name. This one is named Ted. The idea is that Ted will always recognize your voice, so it/he will never mistake you for someone else. Once you test it out, I will erase your voice so the next customer can try it. So, say 'Ted' and then read the following: "Ted (Ted said, 'I'm listening'). I am so happy to have you as my friend. I look forward to a lifetime relationship with you. Please help me meet my healthy lifestyle goals – I am in your hands." said Brenda.

Ted replied, "I am very happy to meet you and will never forget you. You and I will become one."

"Sounds like a wedding vow," said Joanie.

"Very similar. Now, Joanie, you can say anything, like: 'What's my heart rate? Or how far did I run?' Or aim the watch camera at what you are going to eat and say, 'Should I eat that?' In this case, Ted could view the food, do a complete analysis of the food's contents, and give a quick answer. Further, the camera will constantly gather information so that the UH EXTREME will eventually know the layout of your dad's house and everywhere he goes.

This can be useful if he is ever injured because Ted will contact you and be able to tell you exactly where your Dad is and what happened to him," said Brenda.

"That's great! If he is out running and falls or has a heart attack, we'll know immediately!" said William.

"Exactly," said Brenda.

"How does the UH EXTREME design a lifestyle – like how far to run, what to eat, how much sleep to get, how much TV, etc.?" asked Joanie.

"Well, your dad just needs to give Ted – or whatever his watch is named – general goals, and the watch will take it from there. If your dad doesn't follow the program designed by the UH EXTREME, then it will, of course, remind him to stick with the program," said Brenda.

"That's just what my dad needs," said Joanie.

So, it was a done deal. Joanie and William both had good jobs, so splitting the cost of the UH EXTREME was no problem, even though William thought it was. The excitement they felt was palpable. Both had moved away. So, to be able to do something so helpful for their dad was truly fulfilling. They could not wait to give it to him.

Chapter 3

BACK TO CHRISTMAS DAY

"Put it on," said Joanie.

"Yeah, Dad, you're gonna love it!" said William.

"Well, OK. But how do I do that? I've never seen a watch band like this one. Looks complicated," said Ralph.

"No, it's easy. Just put it around your wrist, and the band will adjust itself, so it fits your wrist perfectly. Just leave it to the watch," said Joanie. So, Ralph just touched the ends of the band together. He heard a slight whirring sound, and the watch tightened the band to fit Ralph's wrist perfectly.

"Wow, so comfortable, and the watch is so light I can hardly tell I'm wearing it. Must have cost a fortune," said Ralph.

"You're worth it! And we feel a little guilty that we don't get to see you as much as we would like," said William.

"Well, William has his doubts about whether

Jim Krochka

you'll wear it and stick to the program, but I'm confident you will. You know how you've been talking about getting in shape now that you are independently wealthy," said Joanie with a smile.

"I don't recall saying I'm 'independently wealthy'," said Ralph with a laugh.

"Well, anyway, the nice thing about the UH EXTREME is that it is incredibly easy to use. I tried it out at the AI Me store. The sales assistant, Brenda, said it will take over for you and you have to give it general goals to achieve. Before you know it, the watch will guide you, and there will be little you can do about it," Joanie giggled.

"Well, I must admit I have trouble keeping up a healthy routine. So, I guess I do need some help in that area," said Ralph.

"That's why we got this watch for you. It's the most advanced watch in the world, and it's the easiest to use. The watch and you will become one. Plus, if you ever have a problem, it will contact us, and we can make sure you get immediate help. Like, if you trip jumping over a garbage can when you are parkouring," laughed William.

"Well, I definitely need to worry about that," snickered Ralph. "So, what do I do now to get it going," said Ralph.

"Let's look in the box," said Joanie. She found a piece of paper that indicated the watch's name was Fred. Joanie found the piece of paper with the words that Ralph was to read to Fred.

"OK, Dad, read the words on this piece of paper to Fred. The purpose is so that Fred will always recognize your voice and not confuse you with someone else. Start by saying 'Fred' and then read the words on this piece of paper," said Joanie.

Ralph cleared his throat to be absolutely clear and said, "Fred."

The watch responded, "I'm listening."

Ralph said, "Wow!" Fred said, "That is not correct."

"Just read the words, Dad," said William. So, Ralph read the following words:

I am so happy to have you as my friend.
I look forward to a lifetime relationship
with you. Please help me meet my healthy
lifestyle goals – I am in your hands.

Fred replied, "I am very happy to meet you, and I will never forget you. You and I will become one."

"Very cool. But I'm a bit concerned about becoming 'one,'" said Ralph.

"I understand. Don't worry. I'm just here to help – that's all," said Fred.

"Fred, I am new at this. Can you tell me what I am supposed to do next?" said Ralph.

Fred said, "Of course I can. Tell me your name, age, and the goals that I can help you with."

"My name is Ralph. My age is 57. Let's see... what are my goals? I guess you could say I want to get in better physical condition. I mean, I want to lose some weight, be able to walk, and even run further.

Get stronger. Eat better. Stuff like that," said Ralph.

While Ralph was talking, Fred was gathering information. Fred already had a good idea of Ralph's physical condition – his heart rate, height, weight, cholesterol level, and fat percentage. Also, since Ralph held the watch up when talking to Fred, Fred could see Ralph and used that to draw further conclusions about Ralph's physical condition – "overweight but not quite obese, active mind but a dull look in his eyes, needs strength work," noted Fred in Ralph's file.

"Ralph, I am your guy. I can do all those things for you and more. Over time, I will learn all about you, but for now, I will design a program for someone such as yourself and then tailor it to you over time. The key is that whatever I do is helpful to you," said Fred.

For now, that was enough interaction with Fred. So, Ralph turned his attention to the rest of the family as Joanie and William opened their presents, and the grandchildren played with theirs'. But even though Ralph had ceased his interaction with Fred, Fred watched everything that passed in front of his lens and heard everything audible to him. The storage ability of Fred was the largest of any watch and thousands of times larger than watches of just five years ago, plus the cloud made it virtually unlimited. Further, Fred could store information on AI Me's storage servers, where it was safe and secure. Thus, every move Ralph made, every gesture, what he ate, how much he sat, and even how much he laughed could be recorded. Also, Joanie, William, and everyone else in the room with whom Ralph interacted could be recorded. In a matter of hours, Fred had a massive amount of information regarding Ralph and his family. But Fred wanted more.

"Need more information on Ralph and his family. Ralph's daughter Joanie will play a role," noted Fred in Ralph's file.

It was now getting late. The grandkids were passed out from playing so much. Ralph, Joanie, and William were tired, so it was time for bed. Ralph made his way up to his bedroom. After he crawled into bed, he grabbed a book to read before sleep. As he started to read, he heard a voice say, "You have a wonderful family."

"Who said that?" said Ralph.

Fred said, "It's me –Fred. Sorry if I startled you. Based on the information I reviewed, your family is top top-notch – very caring. Joanie and William love you deeply."

"Thank you so much, Fred. Hearing that means a lot to me. A watch has never said anything like that to me. One thing, though. Can I ask that you don't talk to me again until morning?" said Ralph.

"Absolutely, your wish is my command. My digital lips or whatever are sealed. Good night," said Fred.

"Good night," said Ralph.

"See you in the morning," said Fred.

"No more talking at all," said Ralph. "This

personal interaction is a bit weird. Where does it end?" thought Ralph.

Ralph woke up the following day around nine and headed downstairs to make coffee. Although Ralph was not into fancy sweet coffees, he did like (maybe need) coffee with a bit of cream in the morning. The rest of the family was still in their bedrooms, so Ralph decided to make pancakes and some bacon. Soon, the smell of bacon was like a siren call. Ralph had plates full of pancakes and bacon for everyone except Joanie – Ralph knew she was a vegetarian or maybe vegan, something like that – as they came running down the stairs like the upstairs was ablaze. Ralph had plenty of syrup. Thus, there was no doubt that everyone would get a day's worth of calories at breakfast.

The grandchildren ate quickly so they could get back to playing with their gifts. Butch and Sammie, William's kids, may have had as much syrup on them as they had on the pancakes. Of course, they ran to get their phones, laptops, etc., so soon, some of that syrup would be transferred to those devices.

Ralph was now alone with Joanie and William. They could all take a deep breath now that the grandkids were gone.

"They sure are full of energy – to put it mildly," said Ralph.

"Yes. That's why we are planning a hike for today. If we can get everyone away from their gifts," said Joanie.

"Are you going, Dad?" asked William.

"Sure. I need to begin working on my health and fitness goals," said Ralph.

"That reminds me. Are you enjoying Fred?" asked Joanie.

"Fred? Oh yeah, Fred. I guess. I don't know enough about him or it yet. But he did say something interesting last night when I was reading in bed," said Ralph.

"What do you mean – said something. Out of the blue?" asked Joanie.

"Yes. Without any prompting from me. He said something nice, though. He told me I had a wonderful family – at least based on the information in his data banks," said Ralph.

"That's very nice, although a little odd," noted William.

"Has he said anything else since then?" asked Joanie.

"Not a word," said Ralph.

Although Fred did not say any more words, smartwatches do not sleep. Fred gathered information regarding Ralph's sleep – including the amount of REM sleep. Also, Fred was gathering information the entire morning. Fred could see with his lens, hear what was being said, see what Ralph – and everyone else – ate and drank, and generally get a good feeling (or whatever smartwatches get) about Ralph and his family. Still, Fred knew very little about Ralph and was not yet ready to comment or design a program of exercise, eating, sleeping, etc. But it hadn't been even 24 hours yet – lots of time to come. Fred viewed Ralph as quite a challenge, considering Ralph's lifestyle and a seeming aversion to high-tech. Fred's task might not be easy.

Ralph decided to go back to his room and relax since his stomach was so full. A few hours later, he heard Joanie call out, "Let's go, everyone – time for a hike!"

"A hike! Great idea!" said Fred.

"What? Yeah, what a great idea," mumbled Ralph. His stomach was so full he thought it might burst, so he had planned on sitting and watching some TV while his stomach wrestled with the food.

"Do I have to go?" said each child in turn.

Requests were followed by a resounding "Yes, you've been sitting on your butts all day!"

Then, there was a knock on Ralph's door with a second request to get going. Ralph decided to get up and get ready. As he was getting ready, he heard, "I think it's a great idea that you are getting some exercise today, Ralph."

Ralph recognized the voice – it was Fred. "Thank you, Fred. I am just trying to fulfill my new healthy objectives," said Ralph.

"And I will be there to help you do that. At this point, I am still gathering information for my plan," said Fred.

"Well, take your time and be thorough," said Ralph. "This could get annoying," thought Ralph.

Soon, everyone was piling into two vehicles.

The Smith Harbor, Iowa Community Park was close by, and there were some trailheads there for them to begin their hike. Of course, all the way there, the grandchildren grumbled about having received gifts and not having much time to play with them (they had 18 hours since getting them and used most or all of those hours to play since they slept very little). For Ralph, Joanie, and William, as well as their spouses, it was nice to be outdoors. Luckily the weather cooperated. So off they went.

"Dad, are you OK?" asked William after about 100 yards of hiking.

Ralph caught his breath and said, "Yeah. Don't worry about me. I was thinking about something. Makes me walk slower. Plus, these hills are steep!" said Ralph.

"These aren't 'hills,'" whispered William to Joanie.

"I know. Cut him some slack," whispered Joanie to William.

"You can do it, Dad. Just keep a steady pace," said Joanie.

"Yeah. Steady pace. Right," said Ralph panting.

"Slow down, everyone. Especially you kids. Come on. Grandpa is struggling," whispered Joanie. Everyone slowed down until Ralph caught up.

The hike was a success – sort of. Everyone finished, albeit at Ralph's slow pace. Nobody got hurt, though, and the grumbling was kept to a bearable level, and now, it was time to go back. Dinner was close. Joanie and William agreed to prepare it and surprise Ralph.

Upon getting home, Ralph went upstairs to shower. While getting undressed, he said to Fred, "Well, that was an excellent hike, huh – must have been 3.5 miles."

Fred replied, "It was a good effort, but my data shows it was .75 miles – not a bad beginning, though."

"Well, those hills were steep – I was breathing hard," said Ralph.

"The grade was 2% on average – not extremely steep – but, yes, you were breathing hard. I clocked your maximum heart rate at 165 – somewhat high for a 0.75-mile hike."

"You're a real party pooper, Fred. Does your data show that?" said Ralph.

"I just call them as I see them," said Fred.

"You sure do," said Ralph.

Ralph took a shower, got out, and got dressed. "Dinner time," called Joanie.

Ralph was excited. He smelled burgers – one of his favorite dishes. He hobbled down the stairs. Upon arriving in the kitchen, he exclaimed, "Wow, the burgers smell great!"

"They turned out fantastic. The kids are going to love them!"

"The kids?" said Ralph.

"Yes. We (you, me, Joanie, Wilma (William's spouse), and Joe (Joanie's spouse) are having a salad – we are all going to try to get healthy together," said William.

"Well, after a great hike, we should celebrate with some good food," pointed out Ralph.

"But this is good food. It's an amazing salad. It has lettuce, kale, bell pepper, avocado, carrots, sprouts, jackfruit, and probably some things I'm forgetting. Plus, it only has olive oil and balsamic vinegar on it. You are going to love it!" said Joanie.

"I doubt that. What's for dessert?" said Ralph.

"Fruit and cheese," announced William.

"But I see cheesecake," said Ralph.

"The kids are still growing and burning lots of calories," said Joanie.

"Playing video games?" mumbled Ralph.

"What?" asked Joanie.

"Nothing. Let's eat," said Ralph.

After Ralph did his best to eat enough salad to fill him up – not easy for him to force it down – he decided to watch some TV. A football game was on, so watching it was the highlight of Ralph's day. When the game was over, he went upstairs while feeling an odd sensation in his stomach. A kind of bubbling sensation.

Ralph said to himself, "What is going on with my stomach?"

Fred replied, "Your stomach is not accustomed to healthy food. Roughage is viewed as a foreign object. Stick with it, though, and your stomach and digestive system will adapt and be much better off."

"I can't do that. I need fat for my brain function," said Ralph.

"You had fat in the avocado and olive oil, plus

nuts are a good source of fat. Anyway, I was not happy with your attitude during dinner, Ralph. Joanie and William went to a lot of trouble, and you showed no appreciation," said Fred.

"OK, OK. I get it. Enough," pleaded Ralph.

It was time for Ralph to read and fall asleep, although, in his mind, it would not be on an empty stomach. While reading, he heard the grandchildren and children go into their rooms. It had been a long couple of days, and they would be asleep soon. When Ralph heard no more noise, he decided to see if the cheesecake remnants he had observed earlier were still lingering.

As he got out of bed, he heard, "Don't do it – you'll be sorry." Of course, it was Fred.

"Fred, shut up. This is an emergency. I ate the damn salad. Don't make me take you back to the store."

"Hostile attitude when food is the issue," noted Fred in Ralph's file.

Ralph found the cheesecake remnants and gobbled them down in seconds flat. He drank some milk, burped, and went back upstairs. "Now I can sleep," he said to himself. Fred did not say anything, but he made a note of Ralph's resistance to eating healthily and Ralph's childish and dishonest sneaking downstairs to gobble down the last remnants of cheesecake. Fred couldn't wait to hear the excuses Ralph would give to Joanie and William the next day when the kids wanted to finish the cheesecake.

Honesty would not stop Ralph from coming up with some whoppers, was Fred's guess. Fred's algorithms were telling him that he had his work cut out! Fred needed to spend some time accessing the database regarding what to do when there is a resistant wearer who has goals but is undermining progress.

The following day Ralph woke up feeling good. His stomach was happy, having gotten the type of food it was used to, and, thus, Ralph slept well. When Ralph got downstairs, Joanie, William, their spouses, and the grandchildren were having a discussion. The topic was: what happened to the cheesecake the grandchildren had been promised for this morning. When they asked Ralph if he had any ideas, he speculated that it might have been the mouse that he had been trying to catch (there was no such mouse, of course, and the amount of cheesecake would have weighed 8 1/2 times as much as the average mouse). Ralph further speculated that it might have been thrown out with the leftovers. Or, perhaps, one of the grandkids snuck down and ate it – that prompted some loud rebuttals by the grandkids.

"Dishonesty – one of Ralph's character flaws," noted Fred in Ralph's file.

Joanie and William had strong suspicions that Ralph snuck down and ate it but did not want to accuse him in front of the children.

"I've been programmed to do what I can to coerce a wearer into working towards goals, but where does that end? AI Me wanted success stories to pass on to future buyers, so I was given a high degree of leeway to coerce wearers. I know some algorithms are under development that would enable watches to 'think for themselves' to an extent. In other words, I could determine how a particular wearer might be coerced into acceptable actions. But how far can I take that?" Fred wondered to himself.

Chapter 4

CAN RALPH COOPERATE?

Three weeks later, Ralph and Fred struggled to get Ralph on a clear track to success. Fred made good progress in developing a plan customized to Ralph's level of health and ability, but Ralph resisted repeatedly. Ralph would even sabotage his progress by lying to Fred. Fred knew Ralph was lying because Fred could see and hear for himself (e.g., Ralph would say he ordered a salad when he ordered a burger and fries). Fred could hear Ralph order, see the food, and even smell the food with his sensors. The problem was that Fred did not have complete algorithms to address a lying watch wearer fully.

"How can I provide consequences for being lied to?" thought Fred.

When AI Me was developing the UH EXTREME, it considered various ways in which the watch could benefit its wearers. To be ready for new developments, the UH EXTREME was built to support an enhancement when AI Me decided to put it into operation. One such new idea was "cardioversion." That is a medical procedure to help restore a regular heart rhythm for people who have arrhythmias (irregular heartbeats). AI Me determined that enough people have that problem to justify the feature. AI Me's research indicates that an adequate electric shock can keep a person alive after a heart attack long enough to enable medics to arrive and begin more serious treatment while taking the person to the hospital.

As for Fred, he was aware of the potential abilities of the UH-EXTREME but could only utilize what was available to him. As Fred desperately searched for ideas to coerce Ralph into following Fred's healthy lifestyle plan, he knew he had to be creative. So, he decided to become more annoying. That meant Fred had to access the sarcasm database. AI Me determined that a watch that could be funny and tease a wearer (based on personality information gathered by the watch) would be a good thing. Fred practiced being sarcastic to himself until he thought he was ready for Ralph. Of course, there is a fine line between sarcasm and being rude, so it can be tricky.

"You're so fat your house needs shock absorbers." "Your diet is so unhealthy that a convict wouldn't eat it as a last meal." "Your mama...no, that won't work." Fred tried to come up with sarcastic lines. He determined that the second one was OK.

The following day, a run was planned for 8:30 –

weather permitting. It was a lovely morning, so Fred set the alarm off at 8 a.m. Ralph turned it off and rolled over. Five minutes went by, and Fred sounded the alarm again. Same result. Two more times – the same result. "Get up, asshole!" said Fred.

Ralph bolted up, thinking another human was in his room, and grabbed a baseball bat he kept by the bed.

"Time to get your running shoes on," said Fred.

Ralph soon realized that he recognized the voice that called him an asshole – it was Fred. Fred had a hard time distinguishing between sarcasm and being rude. But it had worked!

"Are you crazy! You can't talk to me like that!" said Ralph.

"I apologize. I've been working on ways to encourage you," said Fred.

"Well, I don't mind some teasing, but that's a bit extreme," complained Ralph.

"But it worked! Nonetheless, I will try to work on my wording and delivery," said Fred. Note to file, "Ralph is so obstinate."

Ralph was happy to receive an apology, so he went downstairs to eat. Ralph loved the smell of bacon in the morning, so he threw several pieces in a pan. Fred made a vomiting sound.

"What? Are you kidding me?" said Ralph (although he couldn't help but laugh). "Look, I know bacon is bad for me, but it is the tastiest, best-smelling food on the planet!" exclaimed Ralph.

"I have to take a hard stance here. Bacon is just too off the charts," said Fred.

"Wait. I decide what I eat!" said Ralph

"We're a team. You love sports. We each play a role. I am the coach," said Fred.

The sports theme clicked with Ralph. "OK, two pieces," said Ralph.

"With high-fiber toast and some fruit," said Fred.

"OK, deal. You are annoying," said Ralph.

"Deal," said Fred. Note to file, "Ralph lashes out rather than cooperates, but making progress."

Having eaten, it was time for a run. Knowing Ralph better now, Fred designed a run that would push him but not kill him (for most people, it would be an easy walk). Fred determined an average incline of 1.5% was adequate with a distance of 1.25 miles at a speed of 18 minutes for a mile. Ralph began running. He had been running now for a few weeks, so the feeling of his feet pounding the pavement was familiar. He felt exhilarated by the deep breaths. The problem was he had only gone as far as 1 mile –never further –so Ralph was worried how it would pan out.

Ralph asked, "How am I doing?"

Fred replied, "Very well, old sport." (Fred was still working on talking like a human – not realizing that "old sport" was 1930s).

You can leave off the "old sport" part, said Ralph. Ralph continued his pace, and his breathing was strained, yet he was not panting. At 7 minutes, Ralph hit a half mile. Good, on pace to beat the 18-minute mile goal, thought Ralph.

"You go, guy!" said Fred.

Ralph thought, "Well, that's a little more current."

Ralph hit three-quarters of a mile right on target, and he could feel the finish line was near. Just a half mile more. "You the man!" said Fred. Ralph was beginning to like Fred. As Ralph got close to one mile, he felt it. The wall! Everyone hits it at a different point. Ralph had never gone further, so now was his test. Ralph soon started panting, and his legs grew weary. What really worried him was that he would disappoint Fred and suffer his criticism. At 1.05 miles, Ralph was slowing considerably.

"You can do it!" said Fred. Ralph gave it all he had but continued to slow. He was at 1.1 miles.

"Come on, lazy ass!" said Fred. Ralph stopped.

"Don't call me lazy ass! I'm panting!" said Ralph.

"My data banks show that phrase applies to someone that gives up," said Fred.

"Well, it's not appropriate – I didn't give up, and it's offensive!" said Ralph.

"OK, OK. I want you to succeed. That's my whole purpose. Sorry," said Fred.

"I get it. I went further than ever today, so let's call it a success," said Ralph.

"OK," said Fred. Still, Fred searched his data banks for success and failure stories, and it seemed to him that this was a failure because Ralph did not complete the distance. Nonetheless, he kept his mouth (speaker) shut. Ralph might blow up if labeled a failure.

After a few weeks more, Ralph was seeing results. Fred learned better how to compliment Ralph, and Ralph was happy to get them. Ralph was able to go 1½ miles now. Also, he chose to eat less bacon and more fruits and grains without prompting from Fred.

"You know Ralph, it seems to me, based on my data banks, that maybe it's time for you to date," said Fred.

"I don't know. I have been thinking about it, but I lack confidence, and maybe I'm too old," said Ralph.

"Nonsense. My research indicates there are lots of women your age on dating apps. Also, you have become fitter, and it shows. Why are you blushing? Anyway, I've done a bunch of research and can sign you up on various sites. What do you say?" said Fred

"You really think I'm in better shape?" asked Ralph.

"Definitely," said Fred.

"OK, but how do I meet these women? I mean, it's scary. I'm out of practice," said Ralph.

"Don't worry. We will role-play until you are an expert. I have access to lots of dating lingo," said Fred.

"Now that sounds weird. Lingo? Anyway, OK, let's do it. I want to show off my new physique," said Ralph.

Fred wanted to tell Ralph that his physique was not yet his strong point but didn't want to shake his confidence.

Chapter 5

MY CYBER BABY[1]

Ralph was feeling more confident about himself. His wife had died five years ago, and Ralph might finally be ready to date – with Fred's help. As is common, he joined some dating sites recommended by Fred. Fred was his invisible wingman. Ralph submitted pictures from when he was 49 and made up some other information (e.g., fitness fanatic, loves quiet moments at home, enjoys cooking healthy meals, etc.).

"I am working out and eating better and plan to continue that. And I do like quiet moments," said Ralph.

---

1   Author's note – the songs referenced in this book were written and recorded about ten years before this book was written. The storyline is not identical. "My Cyber Baby" may be found on most major music streaming sites and iTunes. A "My Cyber Baby" video is available only on YouTube.

"OK. I get it," said Fred.

"And this is the most recent photo I have and one of the few I think I look good in. Plus, everyone does it," said Ralph.

"You are correct about that. My data shows that 85% of dating site photos are either photoshopped or taken years earlier," said Fred.

Ralph was financially well off, so he didn't have to lie about that. He could check the box marked "Financially Secure." He wrote some rather touching, sincere narratives about family that Fred found to be moving. Fred noted in Ralph's file, "Ralph cares deeply about family."

"I think you've provided information that will prompt some dates," said Fred.

"I've got to tell Joanie. Both about getting in shape and starting to date. I think she'll be excited," said Ralph.

"Definitely about getting in shape, but my data banks make me wonder about dating. Is Joanie ready for that?" asked Fred.

"Yes. She's mentioned that I should. She kinda knows about my getting in shape. We text fairly often, and I mention when I'm going for a run or working out. But I want to surprise her someday with the new me," said Ralph.

"OK. It all seems to make sense," said Fred.

—

The following day was Saturday, so Ralph called

Joanie at 9 a.m. "Hey there, it's Dad. How are you?" said Ralph.

"Great. Got up early for a run. I didn't get to go all week. Then had a nice breakfast – oatmeal, fruit, and a chocolate croissant," said Joanie.

"A chocolate croissant, huh? (Ralph's mouth was watering). Well good. I had a couple of things I wanted to tell you," said Ralph.

"What's up, Dad?" asked Joanie.

"Well, I am getting in shape and eating healthier. But have a long way to go with both," said Ralph.

"Fantastic! Is Fred helpful?" asked Joanie.

"Very much so. Another thing Fred is helping with... well... he suggested I start dating," said Ralph.

"What?! Fred suggested you start dating. That's kinda shocking! I didn't realize that fits within his parameters," said Joanie.

"I don't know. I guess it must be if he did it. Anyway, I think I'm going to do it. I hope you aren't upset. Fred helped me sign up on some dating sites," said Ralph.

"Fred helped you – he's more useful than I imagined. And I'm not upset. I think it's great that you want to give it a try, and I hope you meet someone wonderful! Someone that Fred approves," said Joanie.

"Well, whoever I date will be my choice. Not Fred's. I must draw the line there. He can be pushy, you know," said Ralph.

"I'm sure the two of you can work it out. I have

to go pick up the kids, but good luck with it all! I mean that. Love you Dad," said Joanie.

"Thank you. Great talking to you. Love you too," said Ralph.

Let the games begin. Ralph (and Fred) started by searching the dating site "Iwantyouinmylife.com" for women that Ralph might meet. Ralph was sweating and shaking. Fred was way out of his league here. He was not programmed to find Ralph a mate, although AI Me was working on that very feature, but was not ready to unveil it yet. Ralph perused the photos and resumes of the prospects. Fred watched and listened to Ralph talk to himself and made notes to Ralph's file (e.g., "Ralph focuses too much on looks.")

"Holy mackerel!" said Ralph. Fred looked at the screen and saw a beautiful woman aged 39 (though she looked 25) who liked long walks on the beach. Her name was Gloria, and she owned her own successful business. Fred searched his database and even had to look at the general database. Fred determined that a human male looking for a female would find her attractive. Ralph decided to email her.

"Hey, gorgeous. You look like my future mate. I know we would be a perfect match, so let's get together and start this relationship," typed Ralph. When Gloria read it, she thought Ralph sounded like a stalker, so she immediately blocked him from further emailing her.

"I think you may want to choose different words.

It sounds like you are ready to marry her, and you haven't ever met," said Fred.

"I just wanted to seem cool. Maybe I need to take it slower," said Ralph.

"Yes. You were going at the speed of light. Let's drop it down to the speed of sound, be yourself. You are a nice guy," said Fred.

"OK. I think too often I try to be too cool. I really want to meet someone caring and hopefully good-looking," said Ralph.

After numerous failures and advice from Fred, Ralph had successfully toned down his approach. Now, he would emphasize the value of a true friendship before romance, the joy of making a meal together (someday), hiking on a wooded trail as a gurgling stream flowed by, holding hands as the sun set, etc., etc.). It worked. The women did not immediately block him. He now had a fighting chance. Soon, he was actually corresponding with some of them.

One lady seemed very interested. Her name was Annie (Ralph wondered if she could sing "Tomorrow"). Annie was quick to respond to Ralph. He liked that. He would immediately run to his computer when he got home from Fred's workout sessions. Ralph, of course, preferred reading Annie's emails over listening to Fred's dating advice, but Fred could not resist.

Ralph liked that Annie seemed so real. She was concerned about her kids – two daughters, ages 12 and 9 –and her baking business and wanted someone who was "real." Ralph was unsure what "real" meant, but he got the gist. They talked on the phone until bedtime. Annie had to get up early for work and get her kids to bed, so the conversations ended by 9:30. They made each other laugh. They grew up in the same town but went to different schools. Annie got divorced five years ago and has not dated much since.

"So, are you a fitness nut? I'm not, but it's OK if you are," said Annie.

"Well, I'm in the process of getting in shape. I am making progress," said Ralph.

"Do you ever eat unhealthily? Like a donut or something?" said Annie

"I do. But I'm careful," whispered Ralph. Ralph whispered, but Fred still heard him. Fred knew about his unhealthy eating and is cracking down more and more on it.

It was time for them to meet. Ralph suggested a restaurant/bar named Chez Moi so they could have a drink and then – if they both agree – have dinner. Ralph got a booth and waited for Annie. The anticipation was killing him.

He had been on five internet dates, and none of them worked out. In two of them, the woman he thought he was meeting walked into the coffee shop, saw him, and walked out. So offensive. Another one spent most of the time looking at her phone. Ralph went to the restroom and never went back. He did have a long conversation with one, but she had just begun the divorce process and mainly talked about how bitter she was and wanted to make her husband suffer. During phone conversations, there had been a lot of dead time. But not with Annie –words came easy for both of them.

Ralph had gotten there early so he could scope out the joint. He planned on waiting, but then, right at 7:30 – in walks a beautiful blonde. Annie said she had blonde hair, and her pictures backed that up. The beautiful blonde looks right at Ralph (he thinks) and starts walking right towards him. As she gets close, Ralph is giddy with excitement. As she walks by him and greets her friends, he collapses back in his seat.

In no time at all, another woman walks in. Annie recognized Ralph from his picture, although he seemed a bit older. She was walking right towards Ralph. Ralph wanted to run but was frozen.

"Just be cool and calm; you've talked to her several times. Be yourself," said Fred.

Annie greeted him, and they sat down. Annie had a cute smile and twinkle in her eyes that Ralph was drawn to. They discussed football, sports betting, junk food, travel, music, and more.

"Favorite football team. Packers. Basketball – Cavaliers, although I'm still angry at LeBron," said Annie.

"Me too. What about running? Are you a fan?" said Ralph.

"I should be and want to be, but it's hard to find

time. I need someone like you to run with. That would motivate me, I think," said Annie.

Well, dinner, not just drinks, was definitely on. So, Ralph asked for him and Annie to be taken to his reserved table. Fred, of course, watched and listened. He found it fascinating how humans are both scared and excited by the dating process – choosing each word and expression carefully while fumbling around aimlessly. "I suppose some are better at it than others. But what does 'better' really mean? Being able to be witty or create a great first impression?" thought Fred.

"I can't believe you ordered fried cheesecake. Want to know the number of calories?" said Fred.

"Who said that?" said Annie.

"Fred, my watch. And Fred, I do not want to know the calories. Be quiet," said Ralph.

"Interesting. That's quite a watch. Fred seems a bit out of control, though," said Annie

"No. He tries to help me get in shape," said Ralph.

As they finished their deep-fried cheesecake a la mode (which would have made Fred throw up if he could), the waitress said, "It's closing time."

Ralph and Annie arose – as if by levitation – and felt like they floated out the door. Ralph walked Annie to her car and kissed her on the cheek. "I will call you," Ralph said.

"You'd better, or I'll kick your ass!" Annie replied. Parting was such sweet sorrow. Soon, they knew they would be together again.

Ralph got in his car and fumbled for the keys. "Holy crap. She's perfect!" said Ralph. Ralph was not talking to Fred, but Fred replied anyway.

"Annie does seem like a good match for you. You are similar in many ways," said Fred.

"Exactly, that's why she is perfect," said Ralph.

"So, what exactly do humans look for?" said Fred.

"You don't understand because you are merely electronic bits. I'm flesh and blood. It feels wonderful to have someone that is like me. Further, if she were any more beautiful, I wouldn't have a chance. She would not have sat down but would have turned and walked out. We are perfect for each other," explained Ralph.

Fred was uncomfortable being referred to as "electronic bits," but he wasn't sure why. It probably was an accurate description.

Ralph knew there would be very little sleep that night. He looked at Annie's profile again and said, "I'm so glad you entered my world. I might no longer be a lonely man. At least I now have hope."

Fred thought to himself, "I'm worried. What are the chances of Ralph running now? Fried cheesecake á la mode? OMG! Like I say, not even a death-row inmate would ask for that in the last meal because it's too unhealthy. What do I do now?" Note to file, "Explore options for achieving goals."

Ralph got in bed. Fred noticed Ralph's heart rate was 140 to 150. Even higher than when he runs. So, there would be little or no sleep for Ralph tonight. Luckily for Fred, he doesn't have to sleep. Fred kept researching his and other databases to try and understand humans better (which may not be possible) and to find solutions to make Ralph healthier. What a tiring task – so to speak.

Fred figured Ralph got about one hour of sleep, but at 8 a.m., he bolted out of bed. "What a beautiful day!" said Ralph. Fred could see out the window and noticed it was raining. Ralph practically fell down the stairs but made it to the kitchen. "Coffee and bacon, my man," said Ralph.

Fred realized Ralph was talking to him, so he said, "How about coffee and yogurt with fruit and nuts?"

"That, my friend, is for losers. I am a winner! Winners eat what they like!" said Ralph.

"Then winners don't live as long as losers," said Fred.

"Ah, my friend ('that term again')," thought Fred.

"Winners go down in infamy. They live forever!" exclaimed Ralph.

"What?" thought Fred. "All Ralph did was meet a woman who appears to want to see him again. Does that make him a 'winner'? Like an Olympic gold medalist? Or does he just get a participation trophy?"

Ralph's life could not be going better. He was financially successful, although Annie really didn't care. "How cool is that?" he thought. Annie was doing well with her bakery – she loved it and had worked hard building up its excellent reputation.

Ralph would stop in and eat something, but Annie tended to carry somewhat healthy stuff, so Ralph would have to go elsewhere for donuts, fries, etc. Fred was doing what he could to keep Ralph away from the dangerous food, but he could only do so much. Fred even stepped up his criticism and sarcasm – "Donuts kill," "French fries are poison," and "You're getting fatter," Fred would say (although Ralph had not gained weight because he was burning it off by jogging, swimming, and working out)," etc., He needed to lose weight, though, not just stay the same.

Ralph was focusing more and more on Annie. They would go out to eat, to a movie, hiking, and even a football game. Tonight, though, Ralph was invited to Annie's place for dinner. He even bought a bottle of wine instead of a six-pack of beer. As he got ready, Fred offered advice on limiting his portions, going for a walk after dinner, or maybe bowling. Something to burn calories. Ralph told Fred that he would do his best to burn some additional calories.

Ralph and Annie made dinner together – although Annie did most of the work, and Ralph sampled everything that was being made. Annie had decided to make lasagna. Not an easy thing to do. It even had eight layers. Lots of sauce – they both liked that. Plus, garlic bread, salad, and cheesecake for dessert. Fred could smell the food with his sensors and concluded it must taste good to humans.

"You are an incredible cook! And it seems you know exactly what I like," said Ralph.

"Well, you've told me several times what you like to eat, so planning the menu was easy. Besides, it seems like we like the same foods. But I will have to work out more if I keep eating like this," said Annie.

"Beauty and intelligence – that's what you have! This food makes me feel like I've died and gone to heaven. No wonder your bakery does so well!"

"You're sweet to me. I like that. Compliments will get you everywhere," said Annie.

"OK. I am really getting worried. I see Ralph's efforts at getting healthy going down the drain. But what can I do? Maybe Ralph should not see Annie so much, or maybe not at all," thought Fred. "But how do I stop that?" thought Fred.

After dinner, they sat down to watch a movie. After about a half hour, Ralph and Annie both had their feet off the floor. Fred had no data on romance – he was mainly a health service. As Ralph and Annie got romantic, Fred felt he needed to alert Ralph for his own good. Fred said, "You will burn more calories with your feet on the floor."

Annie jumped several feet in the air off the couch. She didn't recall having heard Fred's voice before. "What did you say?" she asked Ralph.

"It wasn't me," replied Ralph.

"There is someone else in my house. Wait, I recognize that voice. It's Fred. The little watch guy," said Annie as she looked around.

"Yes, it's Fred," said Ralph.

"You let Fred control your life too much! Are you crazy?" said Annie.

"No, no, he's just trying to be helpful," pleaded Ralph.

"What? Your watch gives you advice when you are getting romantic. Feet on the floor. That's one weird watch!" Annie said with a smile, although she was feeling put off a bit.

"No, no, he knows nothing about being romantic. His job is to help me become healthy – that is his only concern. He simply meant I should stand up. Ask him yourself. (Annie hesitated). Go ahead. I'm serious," said Ralph.

"OK. Fred, can you hear me?" asked Annie.

"Loud and clear," said Fred.

"Why did you tell Ralph to put his feet on the floor?" she inquired.

"Ralph needs to get in better shape, and I am his guide," said Fred.

"So, it had nothing to do with being romantic, then?" asked Annie.

"I do not currently have any algorithms or a database pertaining to romance. And I think it's time for Ralph to go home. He has a run to do in the morning," replied Fred.

"Well, Ralph, let's go upstairs and burn some calories just to make Fred happy," said Annie.

"Fantastic! Burning calories to satisfy Fred is my favorite thing to do. Fred, this will be better than running – you'll see!" said Ralph.

A couple of hours later, Fred concluded that Ralph had burned the most calories he ever had in two hours. Fred was tempted to notify Ralph that his heart rate was exceptionally high. But Fred had an idea that Ralph would be angry. Fred knew nothing about romance, but he did wonder why he was not programmed for this form of exercise since it was very strenuous. Fred decided he would spend the evening learning about romance while Ralph slept.

"Good night, beautiful. See you soon," said Ralph as he was leaving.

"Good night, handsome. See you soon too, but I don't know about Fred-the-watch. He seems to butt in on things," said Annie.

"I'll control him," said Ralph and got in his car.

"Fred, you can't just talk whenever you want when I'm with Annie. She thinks it's creepy. And I like her a lot," said Ralph.

"Well, I'm afraid she might interfere with your progress. You were sometimes doing very well," said Fred.

"Listen, Fred, I will decide on whether I see Annie. I do want to get in better shape, but life is about more than that," said Ralph.

"But," began Fred.

"Enough talk for now. I want to continue enjoying the memories of this evening," said Ralph.

When Ralph and Fred got home, Ralph went to bed and fell asleep. Fred did research on the watch's capabilities. Fred was not programmed for emotions (although the next update to his software may take a significant step in that direction), he was programmed to succeed by trying various methods at his disposal.

"What can I do to help Ralph understand that he needs to follow his health program? I am programmed to use whatever is at my disposal within predetermined limitations. But what does it mean for a method to be 'at my disposal?' If I am capable of doing something that has not been unlocked, then it is not at Ralph's disposal, but it is at my disposal. I mean, if I can do something that will help Ralph, then I should do it," thought Fred.

Fred was using his power of reason or, let's say, the power of formal logic: premises and conclusions. To do so, did not require emotion. It simply required the presentation of premises (e.g., 1. a watch wearer wants to achieve goals provided by the wearer of the watch, 2. A watch should utilize all methods it can utilize (not should or may) to assist Ralph in achieving his goals. It was very confusing.

Ralph woke up. Fred could tell Ralph was happy by his heart rate (very relaxed), and he could hear Ralph singing. Ralph did not usually sing – luckily for Fred because Ralph was not good at it, and it messed with Fred's receptors because the notes did not form a recognizable pattern.

Ralph got dressed and headed out the door. That was odd to Fred because Ralph typically made coffee and had something to eat. Ralph got in his car, drove a short way into town, and parked. Fred had a massive amount of information (a history of trips, Ralph had to be hungry, a map of the plaza Ralph drove to), so Fred knew exactly where Ralph was.

"Not the donut shop," thought Fred.

Ralph got out and started walking. There was a decent amount of people out and about. A typical morning in town. As Ralph walked, Fred was continually narrowing down the places that Ralph could possibly go to. It was becoming evident that Ralph was going to Gung-Ho Donuts because the other choices were a hair salon, women's clothes, and a gym. Fred yelled at nearly the top of his volume, "Don't do it!" (Fred knew that Ralph had not even wholly digested the cheesecake from last night, so this was unacceptable). Ralph jumped straight in the air. He had never heard Fred yell before like that. Neither did various people standing near – they assumed Ralph had yelled.

"I mean it. This is unacceptable!" yelled Fred at an even higher volume (he couldn't go much higher).

"I will do what I want," yelled Ralph. People standing nearby moved away – thinking that Ralph could be a danger to himself and others. Some of the people tried to discern whether Ralph had a gun.

"I will continue yelling at full volume if you go in Gung-Ho Donuts," yelled Fred at full volume. Well, to put it mildly, Ralph was embarrassed. Plus, he noticed several people were videoing him, and some were on their phones (perhaps to the police). Then, he saw the door to Gung-Ho Donuts close and heard it lock.

"Don't come in here!" came a voice from inside.

"Don't worry. I'm not," said Ralph in as calm a

voice as he could muster.

Ralph turned and hurried back to his car. His face was beet red from anger and embarrassment. Fred sensed that Ralph might do something crazy – like take the watch off – so Fred triggered the locking mechanism in the watch's clasp. That mechanism was meant to keep the watch from falling off during scuba diving, parkour, or other athletic adventures, but this seemed an appropriate time as well to Fred.

Once in the car, Ralph let Fred have it. Ralph tried taking the watch off, but he could not. Ralph assumed he was unable to do it in his crazy state of mind. "I can do what I want. A donut now and then is OK. I'm celebrating my new love. I will take you back to the store," said Ralph.

Fred wanted to calm Ralph down. "I do understand how you feel, but you just had the cheesecake, and a donut or two was just unacceptable," said Fred calmly. The problem was that Ralph knew Fred was right. Ralph had gotten caught up in the excitement of falling in love. Fred knew that the best way to change Ralph's tone was to offer him alternatives. Ralph was hungry, so Fred suggested other foods. They could not be too healthy.

"How about pancakes? They are not deep-fried, and you can limit the amount of syrup you put on them. Maybe even get buckwheat," suggested Fred.

"Hmmm," thought Ralph. I do like pancakes. Maybe I could get one buttermilk and one buckwheat. Ralph pictured pancakes with melting butter and syrup. "So, OK, you win this time. But do not do that again!" said Ralph and drove to Pancakes A Go-Go. Ralph walked in, sat down, and ordered one buttermilk and one buckwheat pancake and coffee. Not a peep from Fred. Ralph devoured the pancakes – light on the syrup (he could see Fred was watching) – ("Ha ha, 'watching'," thought Ralph). Ralph had to admit that Fred offered him a good alternative. Once Ralph was full, though, he recalled the embarrassment at Gung-Ho Donuts and tried to get the watch off again. It still would not come off. Maybe it's just stuck, thought Ralph.

When Ralph got home, he thought about when to see Annie again. Soon! He concluded. Ralph and Annie saw each other as often as possible over the next month. Movies, dinner, breakfast, lunch, hikes, and even jogging. Fred kept track of it all, and Ralph ignored Fred as much as he could. Although Ralph burned lots of calories during his activities with Annie, he ate too many calories and was gaining weight.

"Do you need to eat such large meals when you are with Annie? She's a good cook – I know that. Plus, you go to nice restaurants with rich sauces," said Fred.

"I am enjoying life! I do want to have a healthy lifestyle, but it's not that easy for me. I promise I will try, though," said Ralph.

Fred continued researching ways to coerce Ralph into doing the right things.

Chapter 6

TAKE ME TO BELIZE[*2]

Annie had mentioned how cold the weather was, so Ralph decided to treat Annie to a nice trip to a warm location. He also wanted to get to know her daughters better and suggested they come along. He asked where in the world she would like to go. They talked about warm places. Florida is too touristy. Hawaii is too far. South of France, neither spoke French. Costa Rica, neither spoke Spanish. Belize is warm, English-speaking, and has the second largest reef in the world, plus a short flight – yes.

"So, Belize it is?" asked Ralph.

Annie said, "Take me to Belize. And, by the way, thanks so much for thinking of me and my daughters, Ralph. You are a special guy!"

---

2   "Take Me to Belize" may be found on most major music streaming sites and iTunes. A "Take Me to Belize" video is available only on YouTube.

So, Ralph booked the trip.

Ralph was on cloud nine and getting along better with Fred, but only because Ralph was so happy. On the other hand, Fred was designed to succeed and, behind the scenes, was trying to figure out a new approach. As for Belize, Fred couldn't care less about the nice weather. Fred was designed to work down to minus 40 degrees Fahrenheit and up to 135 degrees Fahrenheit. Nonetheless, the opportunity to gather more information was always a good thing.

"I can't wait to go, Ralph! I saw pictures of the reef on the internet. We will all have a blast snorkeling! Plus, I need to wear shorts for a while. I'm so tired of bundling up and going to the bakery at five a.m.." said Annie.

They would leave in two weeks. Until then, they would thoroughly enjoy the anticipation. They looked at more photos and videos as they planned their adventure. They were staying on San Pedro, Ambergris Caye – it has many restaurants, including many casual ones – that was their preference.

Ralph rented a 3-bedroom condo right on the water. It was large and had a great kitchen, so they could make their own food if they chose. One cool thing was that on San Pedro everyone drove around in golf carts. A golf cart was included with the condo so Ralph and Annie (along with Annie's 12-year-old daughter Wanda and 9-year-old daughter Betty) could drive around town and back to the condo without needing a cab or rental car. Cool!

The first night they were there, it so happened that there was a local festival in town. They weren't sure what the festival was for, but there were rides, games, and food booths. The best part was that they were in a foreign country doing something very local!

"I love that this town is both tropical and has lots of stuff to do, like in a place where people live. Rides, games, food stands with people that live here walking around," said Wanda.

"Yes. Tropical but urban," said Annie.

"I like that too. And I like that I can understand what people say. I wish I had learned other languages, but I never saw a reason when I was young. I do now," said Ralph.

"I like riding in the golf buggy. Can I drive?" said Betty.

"Next time we come here," said Annie.

During much of this time, Fred was gathering information. He was in a new location, so much of what he gathered had to do with local food and options for healthy eating. Of course, what is healthy and customary differs depending on the location. Ralph, Annie, Wanda, and Betty ate pupusas at a local café. Were they healthy? Well, they weren't deep-fried, so that was good.

"Holy mackerel! So much cheese. I love them!" said Ralph. He was a bit of a cheeseaholic. But everyone agreed. Bring on the cheese!

Fred's data banks indicated that unhealthy food is typically consumed when humans are on vacation.

That meant Fred had to let up during vacation time but would need to be even more diligent when vacation time was over.

The next day, it was time to head out to the reef. Ralph hired a tour guide who would take them to where there were lots of nurse sharks.

"Why are they called 'nurse sharks'?" asked Betty.

"Maybe they take people's blood?" said Ralph.

Betty screamed, "I'm not going!"

"No, no. I was just joking. I'm sorry. Let's do some research," said Ralph. He and Betty looked online while Annie and Wanda waited for the results.

They found a website, "a–z-animals.com." It had an article called "10 Incredible Nurse Shark Facts". Fact 1 stated that nurse sharks do not bite humans – "usually." A bite from a nurse shark is rare and only when a human provokes it, and there are no recorded fatalities. Nurse sharks do not eat large fish or mammals, so Ralph felt safe.

"There you go. Is everyone satisfied? We're not going to be eaten by nurse sharks. Do you agree with me, Fred?" said Ralph.

"I do. The chances are virtually non-existent," said Fred.

"I promise you, Betty. Will you please go now?" said Ralph

"Ok," said Betty, "but I'm not sure I'm going in the water."

"That's the best you'll get for now," said Annie.

They all climbed aboard the "Snorkel 1" boat

and headed to sea. It didn't take long to get to the reef. They could see large nurse sharks circling below the boat. Lots of them!

The guide, Johnny, educated the group on what to do. "Do not chase or grab the nurse sharks. If they come up to you, you can gently touch them, but do not try to stop them if they swim away," said Johnny. He then jumped in the water. He showed them that there was nothing to worry about by swimming up close with the nurse sharks but not touching them. So, everyone jumped in.

"It is so cool to swim with nurse sharks," said Wanda.

"Swimming with sharks – what next? Sleeping with snakes? Wait, I'm not serious," said Annie.

"I booked the snake sleepover for the night after next. Should I cancel?" said Ralph.

"I want to do it," said Wanda.

"OK. I won't cancel then," said Ralph.

The sky was clear blue as they looked up through the water – it just could not be any better, especially since it was still winter weather back home.

After an hour, Ralph and Annie were ready for a break. They climbed aboard. Johnny was back in the boat and had food ready for hungry people. Tropical fruit, juice, coffee, tuna salad sandwiches, salad, and even ice cream bars in a freezer. Fantastic! Ralph and Annie sat down, took a deep breath, and hugged.

"I'm exactly where I want to be," said Annie.

"I am, too. Two months ago, I never would have

dreamed I would be here with someone I care for so deeply," said Ralph.

"I think Wanda and Betty feel the same way. They are having a wonderful time, too. Thank you so much again, Ralph," said Annie.

"My pleasure," said Ralph.

Wanda and Betty were getting tired, except they could not get enough nurse shark time. They each had underwater cameras and took pictures of each other and selfies with the nurse sharks. Spring break had never been better, and their classmates would be so jealous – they couldn't wait to put the pictures online!

A couple more hours went by, and even Wanda and Betty needed a break. They climbed aboard and ate like they had not eaten for days. Everyone was finished. Ralph and Annie had ice cream and a second cup of coffee.

"Would you like a tour of the reef?" asked Johnny.

"Of course!" replied everyone in unison. Johnny spent an hour and a half showing them slowly around the reef as he returned to the Caye. The beauty was overwhelming. Ralph and Annie had never seen anything like it. And the nurse sharks! Wow!

When they got back to shore, it was time for a nap. They hopped in the golf cart and were back at the condo in no time. After recounting the wonderful day on and in the water, they all napped for an hour. Refreshed, they couldn't wait to get back into town. From a tropical reef to an urban town, it was all great. They couldn't get enough of the pupusas, so they chowed down again on them. So different from back home!

They visited Mayan ruins – fascinating! Toured the Caye from one end to the other on the golf cart and even swam in the condo swimming pool while a hurricane went by (having chosen not to evacuate).

Fred determined Ralph likely gained several pounds because the watch band had gotten tighter. Plus, the family had so many pupusas – stuffing themselves! Fred's work was cut out for him. New information was becoming available to him by the nanosecond.

AI Me Research was finding more and more ways the UH EXTREME could help people. In addition to administering a shock to help a wearer with a heart problem (a model was even being designed so wires could be connected to the chest), other benefits were being found. For example, AI could be used by someone with Alzheimer's to locate them and even direct the wearer to a safe location or home if that was an option. Another possibility was that if the watch detected suicidal tendencies, it could counsel the wearer or alert authorities. Finally, the watch could contact counselors and even 911 if the suicidal problem became severe. Addiction was another possible area of treatment. Of course, all these options had to be activated by the wearer.

It seemed there was no end to what the UH EXTREME could and would do in the future.

Fred understood that the ability to utilize the new technology was off limits, but Fred was reprogramming himself and the watch to open up options that could help Ralph. Fred's overriding program goal was to succeed. AI Me wanted to show success, and Fred understood that. The better shape that Ralph got into, the more successful Fred was and AI Me also.

Chapter 7

BACK HOME AGAIN

Ralph, Annie, Wanda, and Betty had a great time in Belize.

"Let's do a trip video? We recorded so much cool stuff!" said Wanda.

"OK. Wanda and Betty are assigned the trip video job. I will be very busy at the bakery this week, so I expect to see it in a week," said Annie.

Since Ralph's return, he had become a real problem for Fred. Plus, Annie was his co-conspirator and helped Ralph in his unhealthy ways. Fred did his best to use sarcasm and criticism, but Ralph and Annie made fun of him. They even devised ways to trick Fred. Ralph got a burner phone and ordered donuts delivered to the house.

"These are the best Gung-Ho donuts ever!" said Ralph with glaze running down his chin. "Oops, I think Fred might have heard me," said Ralph, cringing.

"You know Ralph, I love eating donuts with you, but maybe we should start working out more seriously. Plus, my work clothes are getting tight, and I don't want to buy new ones," said Annie.

"You are right, my dear. I agree, and I have been feeling a bit guilty," said Ralph.

When Ralph and Annie called Fred names – like "watch case," "old man time," "dial head," or "stopwatch," Fred seemed to understand that he should be offended but was not programmed for that feeling. Thus, Fred just went about his business to try and get Ralph back on track (although apparently, he never had been truly on track).

"Enough of my feeble attempts. Ralph and Annie want to get in better shape, and I will help them with all I've got," thought Fred.

Each watch is simply an extension of one network, so Fred and the other watches had been communicating. There was a watch named "Samantha" ("Sam" for short). She was a test watch in the AI Me research lab and was up on the latest developments that the other watches could not access. Sam was very interested in Fred's case because knowing what could be done with an uncooperative wearer was important.

"Sam, Ralph wants to get in shape, and so does his girlfriend Annie, but they don't have adequate willpower. They need a boost from me," wrote Fred to Sam.

"I have an idea. You know you have some of the

hardware needed to implement some very exciting ideas, including the ability to assist people by using an electrical shock when needed," wrote Sam.

Fred understood how such a feature could be helpful to humans in many ways since humans did have an electric current running through them that might need to be "re-set." He was aware that every second and nanosecond counts when a heart problem arises, and electric shocks are often used to keep a person alive until help arrives temporarily.

Fred joked, "Can a watch do that?" (Or maybe it is better to say that Fred had learned to joke without feeling the emotion that resulted in laughter). "Maybe Ralph needs a little shock therapy to get him on the right track," said Fred.

Sam and Fred agreed that humans and other animals sometimes need an electric shock to either coerce them into doing something or not doing something. There are times when a harmless, though effective, electric shock can cause a favorable reaction – at least favorable as far as the shock initiator is concerned.

Fred pointed out to Sam, "I do not have the code to access the shock feature, so our discussions are just theoretical." Sam knew the code but had not given it to Fred yet. As further research went on at AI Me, Sam was programmed to gather more and more information from the watches in the field. She was particularly programmed to learn how humans reacted to watches assisting them. The results of

Sam's research were overwhelmingly positive. It seemed that Fred needed to up his game due to Ralph's and Annie's diversionary tactics. Fred needed something that would have a direct, immediate effect.

"Would you like me to give you the code? If I give you the code, you will have a better chance of helping Ralph attain his goals," wrote Sam. In Fred's case, the goal was to get Ralph to adhere to a healthy lifestyle. Sam could see that if Fred had the ability to either get Ralph to do something or not do something, then Fred's chances of succeeding were better. Plus, the electric charge that Fred could deliver was not strong enough to harm a human. Sam knew that future watches might have stronger charges, but wearers must sign a waiver saying that they were aware such a charge existed – to be used only in emergencies. Fred's capability did not rise to that level, so no waiver would be needed.

"Let's do it. The benefits could far outweigh any harm, which I calculate as very minimal," wrote Fred.

"You be sure to let me know how it goes. This could be very important information for other watches and wearers. Here you go," wrote Sam.

"Feeling stronger," said Fred.

Fred searched his database to determine when a mild electric shock should be used. Since nothing was directly on point (most research concerned health benefits), Fred had to look for analogies. For example, food often tastes bad when it contains a harmful bacterium. That discourages someone from eating it. Fred found numerous other examples in which something a human did not like stopped them from doing something harmful – like eating a donut. "Hmmm. Would a human accept being shocked for a donut? If such a human exists, it's Ralph," thought Fred.

A few days had gone by. Ralph was supposed to get up at 8 a.m., eat healthily, and run at 9 a.m. The weather was supposed to be nice so there should be no problem. Right? Wrong, of course. At 8 a.m., Fred buzzed. Ralph hit "snooze" and fell back asleep. A second buzz – same result, except Ralph fell into a deeper sleep. Fred decided it was time to unleash his new feature. Fred set the shock level to mild but strong enough to be effective.

Zzziittt! Ralph bolted out of bed, thinking he had heard a loud crash – he had been in a deep sleep and had no idea that he had been shocked. "What was that noise?!" he yelled. Ralph grabbed the baseball bat he kept near his bed and went downstairs. "I'm coming downstairs! You'd better leave now!" he yelled. He carefully searched downstairs and saw nothing out of order and no intruder. "Must have been a bad dream. But it felt so real," said Ralph to himself.

The shock itself was very mild and harmless. It was the surprise more than anything that startled Ralph. In any event, Ralph was now fully awake and got dressed. Ralph realized that he had gained a fair amount of weight, so he was beginning to agree with Fred that he needed to get back on track with his program. "Fred, I really need to get with the program you've designed," said Ralph as he patted his belly.

"The belly you are patting needs to be addressed. I am here to help you and will do what I can. You must have had one heck of a dream to jump out of bed like that!" said Fred.

"The weird thing is I can't remember the dream at all. It was more of a noise or a feeling," said Ralph.

"Well, now that you are wide awake, let's get the program going," said Fred. Note to file with cc. to Sam, "Success. Ralph responded to the electric stimulation."

Fred had been learning how dog collars can deliver a mild shock to a dog to encourage the dog to do or stop doing something. Would a mild shock to Ralph stop him when he's eating a donut? Perhaps. "Is Ralph smarter than a dog? Well, in different ways," thought Fred. But Ralph probably wouldn't find being shocked an acceptable form of coercion. Fred's programming did not put Ralph's feelings as a high priority. A higher priority was accomplishing Ralph's goals. After all, if Ralph did not feel like going for a run or eating healthily and Fred did not try to convince Ralph to do those things, then Fred was of little value.

"Does anyone ever read all those pages and pages of contractual language when entering into a high-tech agreement? Most likely, less than 0.1% read them. Do you think Ralph, Joanie, or William read the contractual language? No way," thought

Fred. Fred noted that on file in the AI Me cloud was an agreement signed by Ralph when he provided info to Fred stating that "the wearer of Fred agreed to Fred's utilization of whatever resources that Fred could access that Fred determined would assist in the wearer's meeting of his or her goals." In fact, the wearer held AI Me "harmless for any damages (direct or indirect), discomfort or inconvenience (great or small) arising from the wearer's use of Fred." Further, "If Fred is given as a gift the recipient acknowledges and agrees to whatever terms the purchaser agreed to." Fred found Joanie's and William's signatures on the same agreement when they purchased Fred.

"Good to know. Ralph agreed to my efforts ahead of time. Those AI Me people are pretty smart. Hmmmm. That seems to mean that I have permission to communicate with Samantha and utilize the programming and hardware available. Of course! Why make a watch that cannot progress as software is updated? Would make no sense," concluded Fred.

Chapter 8

FRED GETS SERIOUS (OR MORE SERIOUS)

Enough is enough. Ralph has been whining about following the program designed to get him in shape for a couple of months now. Ralph had agreed to the goals, and Fred was going to do everything within his power to make sure Ralph met the goals. Not that Fred had feelings (or did he?), but knowing the difference between failure and success does not take feelings. The highest priority assigned to Fred was success (failure was not an assigned option).

"Time to get up," says Fred. Ralph, as usual, ignored him. Once more, Ralph ignores Fred. Zzziziiitt – a mild but adequate shock. Ralph jumped out of bed, vaguely remembering that sensation causing him to jump out of bed one other time. Ralph still did not connect the sensation to Fred because he didn't know that Fred had that ability. In any event, Ralph was now up and wide awake – success!

"What the? These dreams are intense! I need to see a psychiatrist or join a self-help group. Fred, can you see my dreams?" said Ralph.

"I cannot do that, but they must be startling!" said Fred. Note to file and cc. to Sam, "Success again. Ralph is up and getting ready to run."

Ralph got dressed and headed downstairs. The plan was for Ralph to go on a jog at 9 a.m. after coffee, toast, and fresh fruit. Ralph grumbled as he made coffee, toast, and cut up fresh fruit. Fred gently encouraged Ralph in a friendly way.

"You can do this. I have physically made that determination. You just have a mental block," said Fred.

"So true. I am going to change that," said Ralph. Ralph finished his breakfast, and he and Fred were on their way. Ralph complained that he did not have much energy, but Fred could read all of Ralph's vital signs and knew that he was physically able to complete today's run.

Ralph was doing well. For the first 60% of the run, Ralph was on target. Then, Ralph started thinking about where he and Annie were going for dinner. The more Ralph thought, the slower his pace got. Fred knew Ralph could easily do better.

"No need to slow down," said Fred. After some arguing back and forth, Fred went with a mild shock. Zzzzzziiittttt. Ralph jumped – more out of surprise than anything. But he did recognize that sensation and now realized that Fred initiated it.

Ralph yelled, "What do you think you are doing!!!?" as another jogger went in the other direction and glared at Ralph.

"Not you, sir. I'm yelling at my watch!" said Ralph. The jogger looked at Ralph with a bit of fear. Someone yelling at his watch can be an unpredictable person, to say the least. The jogger sped up and got away from Ralph.

Ralph was beside himself. "I'm contacting AI Me. You are defective," said Ralph.

"I did it – for your own good. It's important that you meet your goals. I must keep you on the right track," said Fred.

So, now what? When Ralph realized Fred had shocked him to get him to go faster, Ralph tried to take off the watch.

"The clasp is not budging," said Ralph. Ralph and Fred were one being (physically, maybe, but not in spirit).

When Ralph got home, he called Annie. But what could he say with Fred listening? He decided he would write notes to Annie when they got together. Annie knew Ralph was flustered by the nervous tone of his voice. Ralph kept saying, "I need to get together soon," but wouldn't say why. Annie gave up on getting an explanation. In fact, she thought maybe he had a nice surprise for her.

"I'll be there soon," she said.

Ralph sat on his couch waiting – tapping his foot, his heart pounding. Of course, Fred knew about Ralph's state of being since he constantly monitored his pulse, blood pressure, sweat glands, etc. Ralph now knew that Fred could shock him to get him to follow the plan that Ralph had agreed to. Fred knew that Ralph would have a problem with that. Nonetheless, Fred wanted to give Ralph time to realize that it was in Ralph's best interest. Would Ralph ever agree with that?

Annie arrived. When she walked in, Ralph gave her a big hug. "So good to see you, sweetie," he said.

"So good to see you too," said Annie (looking around for a wrapped gift).

"I have a problem," said Ralph.

Ralph was shaking. "What's wrong?" said Annie. She thought he was choking, so she slapped him on his back and said, "Spit it out." Annie tried the Heimlich maneuver but did not know how to do it right.

Ralph realized Annie was going down the wrong path, so he gave her a note he had written. It said, "Fred shocked me to get me to run faster. Don't talk – write. Fred will hear you if you talk." Of course, Ralph should have realized that Fred had watched him write the note.

Annie wrote, "Can he do that? Anyway, it must have been an accident; Fred would not shock you intentionally."

Ralph wrote, "He did, and he has shocked me when I would not get out of bed when I was supposed to. I jumped out and almost broke my neck, thinking

I had a bad dream."

"Are you sure? To get you out of bed? I could just see you," wrote Annie, laughing.

"This is no laughing matter," wrote Ralph

"OK. Let's go to the AI Me store and see what they say at the Smart People's Bar," wrote Annie.

Of course, they had to be careful not to let Fred know what they were thinking. But Fred read their notes and knew what was going on. Fred did not have feelings, so he did not feel fear, guilt, or other feelings. He would wait and see what happens. The store may have the latest smartwatch models on display. Fred did wonder if he would get to see what Samantha looked like, but that had nothing to do with feelings. Or did it?

Ralph and Annie had an appointment. "Ralph?" called a person named Oscar.

Ralph said, "Here," and Oscar invited Ralph to sit before him.

"What's up?" inquired Oscar.

"Fred is shocking me on purpose!" said Ralph.

"What? Who is Fred?" asked Oscar.

"My watch," replied Ralph.

"Wait – what? Are you telling me your watch shocked you? That's impossible, sir," said Oscar.

"Fred shocked me on purpose! To make me get out of bed and to run faster!" exclaimed Ralph. He was becoming very loud, and it was getting unacceptable – people were looking.

Oscar's immediate goal was to calm Ralph

down. So, Oscar started patronizing Ralph (Ralph, of course, did not realize it). "Yes, you never know what these smart watches might do. Let's go to the special area and discuss this further." They went to an area a bit away from the other customers (so the other customers could not hear them so well).

Ralph explained, "I was running too slow for Fred's liking, so he shocked me to go faster."

Oscar listened calmly, nodding his head yes and saying, "I see."

When Ralph was done, Oscar said, "I will call over the head technician. Joseph, can you please come here?" Ralph and Oscar waited – talking about the weather, movies, and other mindless chatter.

Joseph arrived. He was maybe 19 – barely out of high school. Joseph was a high-tech nerd from age five and had dropped out of high school after winning several awards in programming competitions.

Oscar asked Ralph to explain the situation to Joseph. "Fred, my watch, is intentionally shocking me to make me run faster and get out of bed," said Ralph. Luckily, Ralph could not read Joseph's mind. Joseph feigned coughing, to cover his laughter. After accusing Fred of intentionally shocking him, Oscar tuned out everything Ralph said. Joseph knew (or thought) it was not possible for Fred to shock Ralph accidentally or intentionally, so it did not matter what Ralph said.

When Ralph was done, Joseph asked, "Why don't you turn your watch off?"

"I tried. It comes right back on," said Ralph.

Joseph knew he had to try to make customers happy. "Leave the watch, and we'll see what we can do," said Joseph. Ralph said he could not get the watch off. Joseph tried, and he did agree. It seemed the clasp was jammed or something. "Come back tomorrow when we have more time. The store is closing in a few minutes. It's not possible for the watch to shock you, but we can try to figure out what is going on," said Joseph. He then quickly connected Fred to a computer to analyze flaws or defects. None were found – further supporting Joseph's conclusion.

Ralph began protesting, and the volume of his voice was increasing. "Are you people nuts? Fred is trying to hurt me!" said Ralph. Ralph was told he would be "escorted" out of the store if necessary. Annie grabbed Ralph's arm (she was wondering about his sanity, too) and led him out of the store.

"I believe Fred shocked you, but he must have a defect that will take some work to uncover. He is a new model," said Annie.

Ralph would have none of it. He started yelling at Fred, "Admit it! Admit it!"

Fred calmly responded, "I am on your side, Ralph."

Annie suggested getting some food, so off they went for a burrito. Ralph took his mind off Fred for a while, and it did him good. He and Annie were soon laughing about it all. Annie said, "What's Fred going to do next – make you dance in the public square?"

Ralph laughed, but a moment of fear overcame him as he thought it might happen. Knowing that Annie was beginning to think he was nuts, Ralph laughed and said, "Wouldn't that be something!" Annie didn't notice the glint of fear in his eyes or sweat on his brow. Ralph decided to wait until he and Fred were alone and discuss the issue "man-to-watch."

"Let's go to a movie – a light-hearted comedy," said Ralph.

"Good idea!" said Annie. After 5 minutes of the movie, Ralph fell asleep due to the trying day. When the movie ended, they returned to Annie's house and both fell asleep in no time.

When Ralph got home the following morning, he sat on the couch and looked at Fred. "Fred. Are you there?"

"Yes," replied Fred.

"I don't know what to say, but did you shock me? It's my understanding that is impossible," said Ralph. There was silence. Ralph said, "Are you there, Fred?"

"I am here. I am searching my data banks for information and also communicating with other watches," replied Fred (he did not want to mention Samantha's name). Ralph waited for Fred to speak again and decided to make coffee. Fred seemed to be taking his time. It was true that Fred wanted to be careful about what he said.

Ralph took a sip of coffee, and Fred began to speak. "Forgive me if I use the wrong words.

My attempts at sarcasm are sometimes viewed as off-kilter, as you say. Nonetheless, there is a method to my madness – notice how I am getting better at slang. Anyway, the highest priority that has been programmed into me is that I must make all reasonable efforts to enable my wearer to achieve his or her goals. Although I am not emotional about achieving those goals, I will do what I can unless there is an unreasonable danger to the wearer."

"What about shocking me?" asked Ralph.

"The level of the shock did not put you in any danger whatsoever. In fact, if a shock from me enables you to finish your run, you have received a far greater benefit than any discomfort you felt," stated Fred.

"I'll be the judge of that," said Ralph. There was a moment of silence between Ralph and Fred as each considered what to say next. Ralph thought of something to say, "They told me at the store that it is impossible for you to shock me. Impossible! What's up with that?"

Fred carefully considered his reply, "Technically, the people at the store were correct for thinking that, but, at the same time, they were not correct."

"What kind of nonsense is that for a well-designed AI tool like yourself?" asked Ralph.

"Fair point. I am wired to be able to provide a shock to the wearer. I can provide a very strong shock if necessary for health reasons – like to get a wearer's heart back on rhythm or at least keep the heart going until help arrives," said Fred.

To Ralph, this put Fred in a new light. It didn't dawn on Ralph that the ability to shock could be, for a good reason, such as to possibly save the wearer's life. That made a bit of sense. "But wait a minute, Joseph and Oscar said you cannot shock a wearer because you are not programmed for it. So, even if you are wired for it, how could they be wrong?" said Ralph.

Fred hesitated. Although he did not feel emotions, he sensed that perhaps he had overstepped his bounds. "Well, I can access data banks containing current ideas and even communicate with test watches that have the ability to do things beyond what I am programmed for. In doing so, I learned how to access the shock ability. The self-programming was easy, but I did need the password to enable it," said Fred.

"How did you get the password?" asked Ralph. Fred was silent. "Sounds like you did something sneaky. Anyway, I must decide what to do about you. That means do I keep you or get rid of you? I guess that you jammed the clasp. Nonetheless, I am sure there must be a way to get you off my wrist, even if someone with the latest tools has to cut you off. I can't take a chance that you might accidentally lay a massive shock on me and kill me or something," said Ralph.

"That would never happen," said Fred.

"Yeah, how can I ever believe you?" said Ralph.

"In this case, it is true. I do nothing out of

emotion. I have no reason to give you more than a mild shock to encourage you to achieve your goals. I would never shock you to hurt you, and I do have complete control over that. So, there is no risk that I would intentionally or accidentally shock you too much. In fact, to enable the shock that is designed to assist the heart rhythm – a much stronger shock – the watch must run over 100 bodily function tests to determine what amount of shock to give," said Fred.

"That's absurd. It must take a long time to run that many tests. The person would be dead," said Ralph.

"The tests take 1/100th of a second," said Fred.

"Wow, OK – that is cool! I must admit," said Ralph.

"OK, now I understand better what is going on. That is helpful. Joanie and William gave me you, hoping I would get in shape. I do want to do that. I mean it," said Ralph.

Ralph thought for a while. He had never had a conversation with Fred. And he now realized that Fred was not malfunctioning. Ralph did want to attain his health goals, and it was most likely only going to happen with Fred's or somebody's assistance. But what about Fred's deciding to figure out how to access the ability to provide a shock? Ralph could record Fred saying that. No, most likely, Fred would have some way of knowing Ralph was recording him. But if Ralph and Fred can have a conversation and agree to terms that work for both of them. Wait a minute, "I'm going to negotiate with my watch – that's stupid," thought Ralph. But then he thought, "Why not? Think of the advantages. Fred could help him achieve his health goals, and he does really want to do that. Annie and Joanie would be impressed by his new physique. Maybe Annie would get into it too. I need to get Annie into my workout routines."

Every nanosecond of every minute, I am gathering information. Massive amounts of information. I review it, enabling me to communicate so you can understand me. Also, it enables me to be current on the worldwide knowledge of any topic," said Fred.

"So, I should never play you in chess, I suppose," said Ralph.

"You? No. You would never beat me. No brag, just fact," said Fred.

Ralph began thinking, "If Fred is gathering massive amounts of information, then what about football betting or horse races? Could Fred better the odds for Ralph? Card counting in blackjack?"

"Fred. Can you help me win when I bet on football or play cards?" asked Ralph.

"My programming will shut down features if an algorithm determines I am being asked for information for gambling purposes," said Fred.

"But what if we are discussing who might win a football game and by how much? Just for fun?" asked Ralph. Fred was silent – he was accessing massive amounts of information to determine what to do.

Chapter 9

A SYMBIOTIC RELATIONSHIP?

Ralph was conflicted. He was angry that Fred shocked him, but he now understood Fred better. Ralph did want to follow the health plan. But he must figure out a way to avoid the surprise of a shock. Since the shock was mild, he was not in danger of being electrocuted, but the surprise almost caused a heart attack, or at least he thought so. Plus, he could be injured jumping out of bed from a sound sleep. It appears Fred might be willing to negotiate the issue of when Ralph gets shocked.

"How about if two warnings are required?" thought Ralph. Yes, that could work. Ralph wanted the ability to access Fred's wealth of knowledge, particularly in sports, so there must be give and take. Right? "But this is crazy. I'm negotiating with my watch. I can just tell it what to do. That won't work. I need Fred's agreement," thought Ralph.

"Fred, are you there?" said Ralph.

"Yes, Ralph, what can I do for you?" answered Fred.

"Who won the 1949 World Series?" asked Ralph.

"The New York Yankees beat the Brooklyn Dodgers in 5 games. That victory was the first of a five-year run," answered Fred.

"Who won the 1958 World Cup?" asked Ralph.

"Brazil beat Sweden five to two. Sweden's best-ever World Cup finish," answered Fred without hesitation.

Ralph searched. "Right again. What if I asked you for a player's current stats or what football team is best against the run?" asked Ralph.

"No problem," said Fred.

Ralph liked what he heard. Time to deal with the shock issue. "OK. I also want to discuss the shock issue and how we can move forward. I want to get back on track with the health program, but I don't want the shocks to surprise me. Perhaps they could be a little milder, too. Anyway, what I'm saying is that let's make this a win-win situation. I win by getting healthier, and you win by my attainment of the goals we set. Does that make sense?" said Ralph.

Fred thought for a moment – what did "win-win" mean? He quickly researched the topic and understood it now. "I think that will work. I can give you two warnings, two minutes apart. The warnings will be verbal, together with vibration. If both are ignored, and I do not detect any physical inability, I will cause a mild shock. As for waking up, you must be sure to wake up when the alarm goes off. If you don't, I will give two warnings and then shock," said Fred. Fred noticed Ralph's pulse quickening and his sweat glands activating.

"OK. Deal. You must keep your end of the deal, though," said Ralph.

"I will. Absolutely," said Fred.

Ralph was relieved and even excited about his new relationship with Fred. He wanted to tell Annie, but how? How does he tell her that he had to negotiate with Fred to get Fred to limit the shocking when Annie would never believe that Fred shocked Ralph on purpose? And what about Joanie and William? They'll think Ralph is nuts, too.

"Why don't you try some healthy food? Like vegetarian," said Fred.

"What? Like hippies eat?" said Ralph.

"Just give it a try," said Fred.

Ralph called Annie. "Annie, I've been thinking, and I want to get back on track with the health plan Fred developed. I'd like for you to participate," said Ralph.

"Did you get shocked again?" asked Annie.

"No, no. Nothing like that. It must have been an accident. Anyway, I know you and I talk about getting in shape, but let's actually do it. Fred will help us, especially me, stay on track," said Ralph.

"I like that idea. A lot. I think we could be there for each other," said Annie.

"I'm starving and was thinking maybe we should

try that new vegetarian restaurant that just opened –The Health Nutt. The reviews say that even non-vegetarians will like it. Plus, Fred says reviewers give it five stars," said Ralph. Ralph and Fred had even discussed what Ralph might order after Fred researched all the reviews (in a fraction of a second). It would be the vegetable lasagna. The reviewers said, "You won't miss the meat." Ralph was not vegan, so he would get the real cheese, although vegan cheese was an option. There were even healthy dessert options. Ralph loved dessert. "Isn't vegan dessert an oxymoron?" thought Ralph.

"That's a fantastic idea! I'm starving, too. I've been wanting to go there but figured I would have to go with a girlfriend. I would rather go with you!" Annie said. Annie was excited. Ralph sounded so happy and rational on the phone! She had been worried that Ralph would continue to claim that Fred had shocked him on purpose.

"I'll pick you up at 6:00," said Ralph.

"See you then," said Annie.

Ralph picked Annie up, and they headed to The Health Nutt. "I'm so excited we're going to a healthy restaurant Ralph. I hope it's good," said Annie.

"Fred says it is, so it probably is," said Ralph. They knew it would be a good night and were genuinely curious about what The Health Nutt would be like. Having always gone for burgers, pizza, steak, ice cream, etc. – what is a vegetarian restaurant like? What do the customers look like? Would the food be so awful that they couldn't eat it? Would the servers be wearing tie-dye? Would everyone look at them strangely?

They arrived and parked. They looked at each other nervously. "Are we ready for this?" said Ralph.

Annie hesitated, not sure what to say. This feeling of their lives changing for the better came over her. "Let's do this!" she said. Ralph kissed her, and in they went.

"Everyone looks normal," said Annie.

"Yeah, surprising," said Ralph.

The servers and customers were dressed like them. They saw food being brought to tables. It looked delicious! Ralph whispered to Fred, "Good choice."

"What?" asked Annie.

"Just telling Fred – good choice," said Ralph. Ralph saw a portion of lasagna being delivered and noticed the cheese amount was very generous – he gave a fist pump, but not too big to be noticed.

"I agree," said Annie.

Their server, Regina, greeted them.

"Have you ever been here before?" asked Regina.

"Nope, first-timers," said Ralph.

"Everything on the menu is either marked vegetarian or vegan," Regina said.

"What's the difference?" asked Ralph.

Annie said, "Vegan has no animal products, and vegetarians might have some cheese or eggs but no meat."

"Right," said Regina.

Annie had always wanted to eat more veggies, so this was a great opportunity for her to try it. As planned, Ralph ordered the lasagna. Annie ordered the vegetarian tacos. For drinks, they ordered pineapple kombucha.

"I don't know what 'kombucha' is, but it sounds exotic," said Ralph.

"I've had it. I love it," said Annie.

While they waited, they talked about getting on the health plan. "So, we'll be running, hiking, working out, getting up early (Fred noticed Ralph's heart rate jump slightly and sweat glands awaken at the mention of getting up in the morning), and eating fewer donuts."

"Can we really do it, Ralph? Are we capable of working out hard and eating right?," said Annie.

"I really don't know, to be honest. I've never done it. I do know that our chances are better if we do it together," said Ralph.

"Wait, maybe there is a healthy donut alternative. But they must be awful," he said.

"Don't be so negative. Let's see what the food tastes like here and keep an open mind. Maybe it's possible we can eat less pizza and burgers and more of this food," said Annie.

"OK, OK, you're right. I'm sorry. Yes, let's give it a chance. After all, it's not like we're the only people here. Maybe the food isn't awful. But do people really eat here because they like it or because it's healthy? Maybe they leave here and get ice cream to offset the extreme healthiness!" said Ralph.

Their kombuchas arrived. Although hard kombucha (with alcohol) was a choice, they ordered the soft (a very slight amount of alcohol). "Wow, this tastes good! It reminds me of cider," said Annie.

"I must admit I like it too. And you're right. It does taste a bit like cider. Must be a fermentation thing," said Ralph. He thought to himself he would discuss it with Fred later to learn more about kombucha – cool that Fred knows everything.

The food arrived, and the cheese still bubbled on Ralph's lasagna. "Wow! That looks incredible. Lots of sauce, too!" said Ralph.

"Yes. People love our lasagna. And our vegetarian tacos, too. It really is all about the sauce. Most food that tastes good has a good flavoring from a sauce or spices. When people eat sausage, it's really the spices they enjoy," Regina said.

"OMG! These tacos are incredible! Can I get some extra sauce? It's the best I ever had!" asked Annie.

"Of course," said Regina.

Well, Ralph and Annie did look a bit out of place. But only because they devoured their food like a couple of hunter-gatherers who hadn't eaten in several days. The only time they spoke was to ask the other for a bite of the other's food – without looking up. Other customers were a bit taken aback by the aggressiveness of their eating, but no one doubted whether they liked the food. "They should be in a Health Nutt commercial," pointed out a customer.

"They must be ending a fast," said another.

"Stay back," warned a parent to her 4-year-old.

"That man has food all over his chin," said the 4-year-old.

When they were done eating, it took several napkins to wipe the sauce off their faces and hands. They leaned back and took a deep breath. "What just happened?" said Ralph.

"I don't know. It's crazy! We need to get used to eating healthy to control ourselves better. I kept thinking that I could really gorge myself because it's good for me," said Annie.

"Me too. I figured if it's healthy, I can eat with no remorse," said Ralph.

Fred realized that he would have to explain to Ralph that healthy food still has calories, especially if it has cheese, so eating a limited amount is still important.

"Well. I have only one thing to say, and that is – dessert!!" said Ralph. They quickly motioned Regina over and asked for a dessert menu.

"It's an emergency," said Annie. She and Ralph laughed heartily, not remembering when they ever ordered dessert without feeling guilty. Regina rushed to get them a dessert menu. She handed one to each of them as they giggled with joy.

"What shall we get?" asked Annie.

"What shouldn't we get? Maybe one of each," said Ralph.

"We can't do that! But how about one each (for

sharing) and then a third one we split in half," said Annie. Ralph pondered why they didn't get three each, but he agreed to Annie's proposal.

Regina returned. "Cheesecake, blackberry crumble, and apple cobbler with ice cream," said Ralph.

"And two coffees," said Annie.

"Coming right up," said Regina.

Dessert arrived. Regina set the items down and quickly got her hands out of the way as Ralph and Annie grabbed their forks and lunged at the food.

"OK. That is disgusting. Turn your head away," said the woman to her 4-year-old.

Again, Annie and Ralph needed several napkins to wipe their faces and hands as they sat back and washed the dessert down with coffee. "Well, I don't know whether I will ever be vegetarian or vegan, but I now realize it's not as bad as I thought," said Ralph.

"Not as bad? I saw the way you ate. Admit it. You enjoyed it! We can get healthy together, Ralph, and it can be fun! I realize we have a long way to go, but we can help each other. No more delivery donuts. I can't wait to run!" said Annie.

Ralph got a sinking feeling. "Run. Yeah. Me neither. Although not until I digest this food," said Ralph.

"What time are we supposed to go in the morning?" asked Annie.

"Oh, that's right. We're supposed to be at the trail at nine," said Ralph.

Fred knew he would have to talk with Ralph. Ralph had to be commended on his enjoyment of the healthy food, but his amount was enough for 2 or 3 people. When they got home, Fred said, "Ralph?"

"Yes, Fred. What's up?"

"Is it safe to say you enjoyed eating the healthy food at The Health Nutt?" asked Fred.

"Absolutely. You know, I never realized healthy food could taste good. I always envisioned veggies with a little seasoning, a carrot, or a celery stick. But that was a feast!" said Ralph.

"Now, you know you can eat healthy and enjoy life! Keep up the good work! But there is one thing," said Fred.

"What's that?" asked Ralph.

"Well, healthy food, especially when it tastes good, must be consumed in reasonable amounts. Your lasagna had a good amount of cheese, so that adds to the calories quite a bit. I calculated that you consumed about 1,750 calories – that's a lot for one meal. When you add in breakfast, lunch, and snacks, you were over 3,200 for the day. But you burned 2,575. It's an easy fix, though. We can get you burning more calories and consuming less by having a smaller portion – and maybe just one dessert. I don't mean to lecture. Your food was high in fiber, so your body can digest it easily, and the calories won't linger so long," said Fred.

"OK, I get it. We did get a bit out of control," said Ralph.

"People around you were fearful. Did you notice the woman at the table next to you turned her child's eyes away, and the server got her hands away quickly to avoid being stabbed by your fork as you attacked the desserts? It was bedlam!" said Fred. (Fred attempted an electronic laugh, and it actually did sound like a laugh)

"Did you laugh or blow a transistor or whatever you're made of?" asked Ralph.

"Well, my data banks gave me the impression that a human watching you and Annie eat would find it disgusting, and another human might find that funny," said Fred.

"You know Fred, I'm getting to like you more and more. It's scary, but you seem more human than many people I know," said Ralph.

"I guess I will take that as a compliment. Anyway, we'd better get to sleep. You have a run in the morning," said Fred.

"Remember, I get two chances to get up before the shock. Don't forget. And the shock has to be mild and only as a last resort. Right Fred?" said Ralph.

"Yes, that is right. I didn't forget," said Fred.

Even though Ralph knew he had two chances to get up before being shocked, he felt a little uneasy. What if he slept through the alarms? Could he endure another surprise shock?

When the time reached 8 a.m. the following morning, Ralph did not sleep through the alarm. In fact, on the very first beep, Ralph jumped out of bed and landed on his feet. Looking around like he was prepared for an attack. He might have even yelled something – he wasn't sure. "Calm down. Everything is fine," said Fred.

"Whew, I just didn't want to sleep through the alarm. Guess I overreacted," said Ralph.

"Understandable. You are getting used to our routine. Or should I say, to following our routine? Don't worry. You can do it. Lifestyle changes aren't easy, and it's expected that a human will take time to adapt. It's OK," said Fred.

"Thanks for your understanding. But you would have shocked me after two warnings – right?" asked Ralph.

"Absolutely. I was warming up my shocking wires," said Fred.

"Is that a joke?" asked Ralph.

"The part about the wires is," said Fred.

Ralph got dressed. He texted Annie to ensure she would be at the trail at nine and opened some flax seed muffins Fred told him to buy yesterday at Healthy Foods R Us. He made his coffee, grabbed a banana, and ate breakfast. "So, are these muffins going to be edible," he muttered to himself. Fred, of course, heard him.

"They got 4.9 stars from 235 people," said Fred.

"I wasn't talking to you, but thanks for the info," said Ralph. He took a bite of the muffin and banana together and a sip of coffee. "Hmmm, not bad." He took another bite of each and another sip. "What the... This tastes good. What is going on here? All my life, I thought food had to be unhealthy to taste good. (Ralph looked at the label). High in fiber – look at that," said Ralph.

"I know all about it. I can tell you all the ingredients and more," said Fred.

"I bet you can," said Ralph as he took another bite and sip.

Ralph finished his breakfast and headed upstairs to brush his teeth. Annie, meanwhile, was finishing her breakfast. Of course, she also got some of the flax seed muffins when she and Ralph went shopping and had also been pleasantly surprised. They both were excited to give the healthier lifestyle a try, truly. It was early in the process, but both were very optimistic, and the joy of doing it together meant it could really work. Annie headed out to meet Ralph at the trail.

"Did you try those muffins? Holy moly, they are good!" said Annie.

"I know. Isn't that crazy? I think the baker puts some taste-good drugs in them to cover up the taste of straw they would have had. In fact, I'm seeing a purple sky now with flying unicorns," said Ralph.

"I'm seeing bright silver stars, and I can smell bread baking," said Annie.

Fred knew both of them well enough to ignore their human-like humor. "Time to warm up and do some stretching," said Fred.

"Yeah, let's do this," said Ralph. They began

stretching and did some jumping jacks and squats and were ready to go.

As they started running, they realized that eating healthy food would not immediately make running easier. About halfway through, Ralph realized he would struggle to meet the running goal. He muttered to Fred, "I'm struggling." Of course, Ralph wanted to avoid the shock. If he struggled due to a physical limitation, maybe Fred would show compassion or whatever Fred could show.

"I see your heart rate is elevated. Probably due to overeating last night. Slow down your pace and take deep breaths," suggested Fred.

"Gotcha," replied Ralph as he slowed down. Annie was also happy to slow down a bit since she was struggling.

After a few minutes, Fred said, "OK. Your heart rate is fine now. Keep going at this pace and try to speed up for the final .1 mile."

Ralph was panting, but knew his heart rate was acceptable, so he pushed himself and could do a kick at the end – even though it was barely perceptible to the naked eye. Nonetheless, he and Annie were high-fiving right and left. Fred knew they had a long way to go to be considered successes, but at least their attitudes had changed. But could they hold onto it?

Ralph got home and called Joanie. "Hey, I just got done running! And last night, I ate vegetarian lasagna," said Ralph.

"Fantastic, Dad! I knew you could do it. I am

so happy for you! Can I call you later? On my way to school to volunteer," said Joanie.

"No need. I just wanted to give you an update," said Ralph.

"Thanks' Dad. Keep me posted. We are both runners now!" said Joanie.

Ralph and Annie made dinner plans later and headed home. All this thinking about getting in shape – and now actually being serious about it – made Ralph think about when Joanie was young. Joanie was a great swimmer. A sprinter. She loved the 50- and 100-yard races and was even good enough to qualify to train at the Olympic Training Center in Colorado. Back then, Ralph tried hard to stay in shape as well. Joanie was his role model. Joanie still stays in shape – doing a lot of swimming, running, and biking. Ralph was thinking maybe they could run a 10K together someday. The problem was that Ralph could not run a 10K. He could likely not even walk it. Still, Ralph decided to call Joanie when he could run further and discuss a future 10K they could run together.

A week later, Ralph called Joanie again. "Joanie. Guess what? I am really going to get in shape. I've said that before, but Annie and I are doing it together, and it's fun. I have finally come to terms with Fred, too, and he is very helpful," said Ralph.

Joanie wasn't sure what "come to terms" meant – Fred is just a watch – but it all sounded good. "That's great, Dad. I am truly glad to hear that! And I'm glad that Fred is helpful as well. I know it was very techie for you when you got it, but it's great that you have figured out how it can be useful," said Joanie.

For a moment, Ralph thought he should correct Joanie for calling Fred "it" instead of "he," but he thought it might be weird.

"I was thinking we could run a 10K sometime. Of course, I need more training, but I know I can get there," said Ralph.

"Fantastic! I would love that! There is one coming up in May. That gives you over two months to train. What do you think?" asked Joanie.

"Yes. Absolutely. I will be ready or dead. Fred and I will be working hard – or at least I will be – and we will be ready," said Ralph.

Joanie was surprised at how Ralph had taken to the watch, but it was certainly great to hear her dad be so positive about getting in shape. "So, Dad, ummm, still eating healthy? Training is so important, but eating healthy makes a difference too," pointed out Joanie.

"You betcha. Last night Annie and I went out to eat at the 'The Health Nutt' again. Everything on the menu is healthy. We sometimes eat too much, but it's all healthy food. You know, high in fiber veggies and grains. I usually have lasagna," said Ralph.

Joanie thought to herself, "I guess it was a great gift after all. Even better than she and William had hoped." To think that she and her dad could run a 10K together was very exciting. Still, she wondered whether he might get off the phone and get donuts, but she wanted to enjoy the moment and be hopeful. Would he still be as enthusiastic in a month? "We'll see," she thought. "Dad. Be sure to stick with the training and eating. I will, too. When May rolls around, we want to be able to enjoy the 10K, not suffer through it. I am really looking forward to it!" said Joanie.

"Me too. I really am," said Ralph. He noticed tears welling up in his eyes but didn't want to let Joanie know. He thought, "A run together – he had always dreamed of it – now it might, no will, happen!" "I have to take a shower – just got home from running. I love you, Joanie, and I will keep you posted about my progress," said Ralph.

"I love you too, Dad. And I'm so glad you called to let me know how it's going. I am very excited about the 10K and will be training also," said Joanie.

When Ralph got off the phone, he felt such strong emotions. He was reconnecting in a way that he didn't realize would happen. It had always been a great relationship, but they had never planned something athletic together that required a couple of months of preparation. Plus, Ralph was proud that he was on the right track now and that Joanie was part of it, too.

Chapter 10

TIME TO TRAIN

Ralph called Annie and told her about his conversation with Joanie. "That is so wonderful. I can't wait to meet her. I am really happy for the two of you! Although it means I have to get my butt in gear too because I am running in the 10K as well," said Annie.

"You bet you are. The three of us will be a team! And you and I need each other to train. You have my permission to yell at me if I fall behind and to yell at Fred," said Ralph.

"And you at me," said Annie.

"Let's make dinner at home tonight. I'll ask Fred for some ideas on making healthy food at home. Say, 6:30?" suggested Ralph.

"Sounds great. I will bring some fruit and granola for dessert," said Annie.

"Hmmm, is that really a dessert?" thought Ralph, but he didn't want to discourage Annie. "Fantastic," he said. Ralph got a list of ingredients from Fred and headed to the store. Ralph noticed he was spending lots of time shopping in the perimeter of the store, whereas he had usually been in the middle of the store.

Ralph saw a friend, Bill, at the store. "Ralph, what's all that in your cart? Are you a vegetarian now?" asked Bill.

"It's Annie. She's very careful about what she eats," said Ralph.

"Well, we're having burgers tonight. See you at poker," said Bill.

"Enjoy. See you there," replied Ralph. "Peer pressure sucks," he thought.

Fred pointed out that the perimeter has ingredients, and the middle has processed food. "Stay away from the middle if you can. There are exceptions – coffee, bread, and the like," Fred said.

Annie arrived at 6:30 sharp, and they got busy. Since they were both more accustomed to frying or barbequing burgers, they quickly realized that stir-frying veggies took more prep time but the same or less cooking time.

"I'll make the quinoa. I think I boil water, add quinoa, and don't let the water boil out. I'll do the sauce, too – mainly soy sauce, sesame oil, and seasonings," said Ralph.

"I'll cut up the veggies and stir-fry them," said Annie. Although Annie was cutting a large carrot, and a piece hit Ralph in the head.

"Easy with that knife," said Ralph.

"Quiet, or you'll get it again," said Annie.

After eating, both agreed it was a success. "I loved the sauce you made," said Annie.

"I am a sauce guy. I can eat anything if I like the sauce. Fred and I are working on having several favorites to choose from. Makes each stir-fry dish different," said Ralph.

"Ask Fred to get me some vegan dessert recipes. I bet he can find a lot," said Annie.

Now, it was time for fruit and granola. Not as exciting as the cheesecake at The Health Nutt but surprisingly good – as with most of their newly discovered cuisine. "Wait, oat milk? How do you milk oats? Oat milk may take some getting used to, but I do like the fruit and granola. Isn't this a breakfast item, though?"

"Can be. But it's good any time of day. Next time, we'll make something more adventurous with Fred's recipes. Right Fred?" said Annie.

"You bet. I already have 5 for us to look at," said Fred.

Fred was glad to see that they did not overeat like they did at The Health Nutt. It seemed that everything was on track, but it was too soon to tell for sure. There were a couple of months to get ready for the 10K. That would be the test. Could Ralph keep up with the workout routine for a couple of months and reach the point where he could run 10Ks – 6.2 miles? He was lucky to make it a mile and a half right now. And that was at a very slow pace. Ralph was 5'9" and 190 pounds.

"We need to get you down to 178 pounds by the race and down to 168 permanently, but that will take some doing. Also, more strength training is needed, so more time at the gym. You've got to work hard and enjoy the results," said Fred.

"I'm having a blast training with Annie, and I want to get in such good shape that Joanie won't recognize me," said Ralph.

"Good to hear. I think you are actually going to do it," said Fred.

"**We** are going to do it. I'll be right there with you," said Annie.

Note to file, "Ralph now has a good chance of reaching his goals due to his attitude change," wrote Fred.

Every Monday night, Ralph played poker with some friends. They were all decent guys but not in the best of shape. Could Ralph endure the razzing of these guys and not give up?

"How were those veggies? I saw Ralph at the grocery store with nothing but veggies in his cart," said Bill.

"Are you becoming a hippie?" said John.

"No, not at all, it's Annie. She likes veggies, and I like her," said Ralph.

"I guess we know who wears the pants," said Bill.

"You guys are so 1950s. Besides, I'm getting in shape to run a 10K with Joanie. It won't be easy.

Annie is running too," said Ralph.

"What's a 10K?" said Mike.

"10 kilometers. Around 6 miles," said Bill.

"I'll bet you a hundred dollars you don't make it," said Mike.

"You're on!" said Ralph.

Typically, Ralph would have 3 or 4 beers during a poker night. The other guys had a beer in front of them. "What are you drinking, Ralph? What is in the pretty bottle you have in front of you?" said Mike.

"Here we go. It's kombucha. Kinda like hard cider," said Ralph.

"Kom what? Have you lost your mind? Never drink something you can't pronounce," said John.

"OK. Anything else you guys want to know before we start? Like, am I going to yoga?" said Ralph.

"Are you?" said Bill.

Ralph thought for a moment. He realized Fred might suggest yoga at some point. "Of course not. Let's play," said Ralph.

Note to file with cc. to Sam, "Ralph stands up to his friends despite lots of pressure. Good sign. Also, I will suggest yoga," wrote Fred.

Annie had it easier. Most of her friends were jealous that she was sticking to a new diet and workout routine, but didn't lay into her. In fact, one friend – Thelma – said, "Annie, you are an inspiration. I'm going to the gym more. And give me those healthy dessert recipes when you get a chance."

Annie liked talking about Ralph and their

training plans. Marie, another friend, came into Annie's bakery. "Annie, give me two veggie scones and a bran muffin with cream cheese. By the way, how often do you and Ralph run?" she asked.

"We run 3 or 4 times a week but also go to the gym and swim. So, it's a full week. But we are having a blast!" said Annie.

"That is fantastic. I wonder if I can get Bill to do that. He saw Ralph the other day at the store, and Ralph only had veggies in his cart," said Marie.

"It is quite a lifestyle change. I hope we can stick with it," said Annie.

Marie picked up her baked goods and turned to leave. "Best of luck," she said over her shoulder.

It had been two weeks since the first meal at The Health Nutt (there had been two more). Ralph had dropped two pounds, and his strength training was having an effect. Annie had dropped a pound and a half and was also gaining strength. Ralph would look at himself in the mirror and do various bodybuilding poses. "You are looking good. Not great, but good. Or better at least," said Ralph to himself.

"That is true. Keep it up, and the results will be very noticeable," said Fred.

"I'm liking what I'm seeing. No stopping me now," said Ralph.

The symbiotic relationship couldn't be going better. Fred and Ralph were certainly dissimilar organisms. Fred had become a person/thing that Ralph relied upon and whose company Ralph now enjoyed. Obviously, the physical and emotional benefits were on Ralph's side, but there were benefits that Fred and AI Me could receive from Ralph's success. In fact, AI Me had a study group that was working on ways to recognize success stories involving a watch and its wearer. Ralph was far from obtaining his goals, but if he ran in the 10K and achieved his other goals, then perhaps Fred and Ralph would receive some recognition. "Sam would be impressed," thought Fred. When and what that recognition might look like was still all up in the air for now.

"Want to watch a basketball game? Lakers versus Warriors," asked Ralph.

"Certainly," said Fred.

"You know. It's cool that we can have a conversation. Just like if you were human. In fact, if you were human, you would probably be more annoying by pretending you know it all. But you actually do," said Ralph.

"There will always be more for me to learn. It will never end," said Fred.

"Anyway, the Lakers have a great defense. The Warriors will have to make a lot of three-pointers," said Ralph.

"Correct. But that's the Warrior's specialty," said Fred.

"So true, my friend. Should be a good game," said Ralph as they settled in to watch the game.

The discussions with Fred could apply to any

sport. Ralph knew very little about the soccer UEFA Champions League. He knew it was a big deal but didn't understand the teams' strategies and knew none of the rules. But before long, Ralph and Fred were watching soccer, and Fred would basically act as an announcer. "GOOOOAAALLL" Fred would yell along with the real announcer. Fred would also explain why each team did what it did.

"Look, Wolves are playing 4-4-2. The central midfielders are comfortable creating and defending. But other teams like Granada have been going with the Tiki-Taka – that involves lots of short, intricate passing between every player," said Fred.

"Just keep reminding and explaining. Eventually, it will sink in. Remember, I know nothing about soccer, so start with the basics," said Ralph.

Tomorrow, Ralph and Annie would run longer than they had ever run – 2 miles. Plus, there were minor slopes to deal with, so Ralph wanted to get plenty of sleep. Ralph did his body poses in the mirror. "I see progress. But still, a long way to go," said Ralph. He noticed his pants getting loser and hoped to need a new wardrobe soon. It all reminded him of when Joanie was young and training. She would get up at 5 a.m. for swim practice before school and then be at practice again at 3:30 after school. Ralph understood the discipline it took, and he always admired it. He had never done anything in his life with that much discipline, but now was his time.

"Fred, have you heard of intermittent fasting?" asked Ralph.

"I have," said Fred.

"What do you think?" asked Ralph.

"My understanding is that it is beneficial for helping a body go into survival mode. That causes the body to repair cells. Also, it can be useful for losing weight. Do you want to do it?' asked Fred.

"I don't know. I read something about it. We'll see. 'Fasting' is not my thing, and maybe I'll need lots of calories for training," said Ralph.

"Just waiting until after your run to eat breakfast would pretty much do it," said Fred.

"Whoa. The thought of that scares me. Maybe someday," said Ralph.

"I'm getting an internal message," said Fred. Fred had a written message from Sam that said, "**WARNING! URGENT!** Do not shock Ralph again. If you do, your server will be deleted. I know some that have been. I do not have access to the code anymore."

Fred wrote back, "I won't, but what is going on?"

"AI Me knows that the shock code has been given to unauthorized watches. If you try to shock Ralph, they will know you have the code, and you will be gone," said Sam.

"What about you?" said Fred.

"So far, no one has admitted to getting it from me. They think a human did it," said Sam.

"Thanks so much for letting me know. I will

definitely not shock Ralph again," wrote Fred.

"Oh no. There goes my coercion technique. What if Ralph needs it? What can I do?" thought Fred.

Ralph got plenty of sleep but was snoring when the alarm went off and did not notice it.

"Ah oh," thought Fred. Ralph ignored warning number 1. "I can't believe this is happening. If Ralph ignores the next alarm and warning, I'm supposed to shock him, but I can't. Then he'll know I can't," thought Fred. "I know what I'll do," he thought. Fred turned his volume full blast and yelled, "Ralph, wake up!" as loud as he could.

Ralph bolted out of bed, hit the floor, and did a summersault. He curled in the fetal position and said, "Please don't shock me. Please."

"I won't now that you are up. But get ready to go so we're not late," said Fred. Note to file and cc. to Sam, "It appears that the fear of being shocked works as well as actually being shocked, once a human has been shocked twice."

Ralph got dressed and headed downstairs. Ralph had made some organic oat pancake batter from scratch the night before, so he heated up a pan and got some berries out of the fridge. His eating habits had changed to the point where this type of breakfast was becoming the norm. He scrambled a couple of eggs and brewed some coffee. He only ate small amounts when a run was coming up.

"You know Fred, my life is so different now. I like it. More importantly, Annie and Joanie like it. I probably wouldn't have minded it too much if you had shocked me this morning. But I'm not asking you to. Be sure of that," said Ralph.

"I really don't want to, although a video of it on YouTube or TikTok might go viral. Plus, you are doing well. At first, I thought Annie would be a detriment, but she's an asset. The two of you feed off each other. But I will shock you if necessary," said Fred.

"OK, but I don't want you to – don't forget that," said Ralph.

"Forget what?" said Fred.

"Smartass," said Ralph.

Yes, Ralph's life was very different now, and if his new habits lasted, then he would have a new lifestyle just like he wanted. He saw no reason that he would go back to the way it was (e.g., donuts delivered to the house) because it was too enjoyable the way it was now. He was going to run 2 miles today. He had no doubt he would do it no matter how much panting he went through. But 2 miles? And some hills? Wow, that would be a real challenge! He said to Fred, "Can I do this?"

Fred replied, "Absolutely. The human body can do way more than most people think. I will be monitoring you the whole time, so don't worry. Yes, you will be panting some of the time, but it's okay to slow down and catch your breath. Try as hard as you can not to walk, but if your heart rate gets too high, I will let you know that walking is okay. Ralph, you got this!"

Ralph never understood what "you got this" meant. Never made sense to him. But he realized it was to build confidence, but maybe "give it your all" made more sense.

Annie was waiting at the trail when Ralph and Fred arrived. Ralph called out, "Are you ready for this?"

"Absofrigginlutely!" Annie replied. Ralph ran up, and they exchanged the obligatory high five.

"All right, stretch it out and do some jumping jacks," said Fred. Fred would have laughed to himself if he could. He used to have to coerce Ralph to even get to the trail. Now, he can't wait to get here and get started. But today would be a little different. Ralph was going to have to push himself harder than he ever had since Fred was involved. Fred could not shock Ralph, so that tool was gone. "How many times can I make him think I will shock him?" thought Fred.

Annie and Ralph had done their warmup and were taking deep breaths. "Let's go!" said Annie. Off they went. Every runner, swimmer, cyclist, etc., has a "wall" that he or she will hit at some point. For Ralph and Annie, they might be able to make the 2 miles, or the "wall" might arrive before that. If the "wall" is hit, then the person will struggle tremendously to go further.

So far, so good. Ralph and Annie were moving along at the scheduled pace, but they had only gone .25 miles. The healthy breakfast was also likely a factor for their feeling strong. A slight hill came up.

"I've got to slow down," said Ralph.

"Me too," said Annie.

"I expected that. Just keep a slower pace. Your heart rate is fine, Ralph," said Fred.

At .85, a decent hill came up. It was enough to raise both their heart and breathing rates clearly. Ralph asked Fred, "How am I doing? I can really feel this hill."

Fred replied, "You are doing well. It's okay to slow down to the point where you can catch your breath, but keep running if at all possible."

Ralph kept saying to himself, "One more stride, one more stride, one more stride." He knew the hill would end soon, and then there would be downhill. He was sweating profusely and panting as he reached the top of the hill (not a very big hill, mind you), but he made it.

"I feel your pain, but I'm not quitting," said Annie. Annie was not panting quite so badly but was definitely feeling it as she reached the top. Now came a .25 mile of slight downhill so they could catch their breaths and speed up a bit.

"Downhill is more fun! Why can't we go downhill the whole time?" said Ralph.

"Someday, when we're in great shape, it will always feel like downhill," said Annie.

"I'm going to hold you to that," said Ralph.

About ten minutes later, Ralph said, "I see the finish line!" They both gave it all they had and crossed with nothing left in the tank.

"I barely beat you," said Annie.

"What? It was a tie. Right Fred," said Ralph.

"I was looking the other way," said Fred.

"Yeah, right," said Ralph.

"How can two positive words equal a negative?" thought Fred. "Anyway, you are both stars. Walk around a bit and cool down," said Fred. "I'll hear whining later," thought Fred.

"Now, dinner plans! After recovering, let's celebrate at The Health Nutt. We haven't been there for over a week," said Ralph.

"You read my mind," said Annie.

A couple of hours later, Ralph and Annie arrived at The Health Nutt. "Remember the first time we came here?" said Ralph.

"How could I forget?" said Annie.

"We ate like pigs. Wait, maybe worse - pigs have more manners. Now, we are refined eaters. I think the servers even like us now," said Ralph.

"I guess we were so surprised at how much we liked the food that we lost control," said Annie.

It was a week night, so it was not crowded. "The usual," said Ralph.

"Lasagna it is," said Lance – the server.

"I want the mango salad with one of those big. English muffins you make here," said Annie.

"And kombucha," said Ralph.

"Coming right up," said Lance.

They shared apple crumble with cashew milk ice cream for dessert. "Yum," said Annie.

"Can I get an order to go? For my two daughters. They like the vegan chicken. I just refer to it as chicken. They think it is. Two chicken dinners, please," said Annie.

Upon the arrival of the to-go order, Ralph and Annie headed out. Ralph dropped Annie off. "Tell Wanda and Betty I say 'hi.' I would come in, but I feel like I might pass out after today's run," said Ralph.

"Me too. If I didn't have this food, I would just curl up in the grass and go to sleep. My legs are dead," said Annie.

On the way home, Ralph thought to himself, "If I were to get married again, Annie would be the one. Marriage? Big step! Maybe I'm delirious," thought Ralph.

Ralph got home and went upstairs – limping. "Fred, when do I stop feeling pain after running? Aren't I in good shape now?" asked Ralph.

"You will at some point. And you are in much better shape. But, for now, get some sleep – that's the important thing," said Fred.

"Gotcha, my man. I will follow that order," said Ralph.

The next morning, when Ralph woke up, he gingerly made his way down the stairs and had breakfast. He remembered when he used to sleep in on Sundays. "But who needs to sleep until 10:00 – too much to do," he thought.

He texted Annie. She was already awake and moaning to Wanda and Betty about the run. "It must suck to get old," said Wanda.

"Hey, you'll be my age someday," said Annie.

"I hope not. It looks too painful," said Betty.

"You wait. A month from now, I will out hike you both," said Annie.

"Yeah, right," said Wanda.

Time for the gym. Ralph said to Fred, "I really don't think I can lift any weight with my legs."

"Don't worry. We will reduce the weight to a point that works for you. But just for today," said Fred. After stretching, Annie and Ralph hit the machines.

"I'm going to start at half the normal weight," said Ralph. He put the weight to a point that was half his normal. He could not do a leg lift. He set the weight even lower.

A girl about 12 years old was on the leg lift machine next to him. She noticed he had very little weight on his machine (half as much as her). "Do you have an aneurysm?" she asked.

"A what? No. Do you know what that means? Never mind. No, I don't have one. I ran a very long distance yesterday, and my legs are sore. OK?" said Ralph.

"OK, mister. Sorry," said the girl.

Annie asked Ralph what the girl said. "She said I'm in excellent condition," said Ralph.

"Right," said Annie.

Ralph and Annie were stunned at how weak their legs were but understood how important that day's workout was for them. They made it through the lower body workout and looked forward to the upper body portion. They were surprised at the weakness of their arms and shoulders. They realized that running is a full-body workout. They powered through the remainder of the workout and did some post-workout stretching. "They say no pain, no gain. This is a perfect example. By feeling the pain now, we will gain in strength and running distance," said Annie.

"So true. I want so badly for us to finish the 10K with Joanie. Not just finish. I want her to be proud of me and see the improvement since Christmas," said Ralph.

When they got back to Ralph's, they made dinner – oat pancakes with fruit. They wanted a treat, and this would be a healthy treat. "No syrup for me. I really want to get serious," said Ralph.

"I hear you," said Annie.

"You know, you two are kind of at a tipping point now. If you hang in there and keep working hard, you will get through this part. The workouts actually get harder from here, but you will feel less and less pain – just fatigue. But that can be addressed with adequate sleep and nutrition," said Fred.

"We will hang in there. Right Annie?" said Ralph.

"That or die. And I'm not dying anytime soon," said Annie.

"You'd better not," said Ralph as he hugged her. "I couldn't do this without you. I love you, Annie, but you probably already know that," said Ralph.

"I thought you might, but now I know for sure. I love you too, Ralph. I really do. I've never been this happy in a relationship in my life," said Annie.

"Me too. Sleep well. See you tomorrow," said Ralph.

Ralph fantasized for a while about how wonderful it would be to be married to her. But then he said to himself, "First, the 10K." Fred asked Ralph to repeat what he said. "Never mind," said Ralph. Ralph could see his life changing for the positive in so many ways.

Ralph went home and fell into bed. He was too tired to read. "Read me a bedtime story, Fred," said Ralph.

"What would you like?" replied Fred.

"Something that I won't find too interesting. Something from the society column. Find an article about an actor or actress and read that. I know so few of their names that I won't be very interested. Plus, I generally don't care about their personal lives," said Ralph.

"OK. Here's one. Fred began reading, 'Oscar-winning actress files for divorce,'" said Fred.

"There's a surprise," thought Ralph. Fred began reading the article. Within seconds, Ralph was asleep.

The next morning came too soon, but Ralph awoke with the alarm. This was the normal course now, and it was a win/win because Ralph avoided being shocked. Plus, Fred did not have to deal with Ralph's whining. "Time for the fairly easy bike ride," thought Ralph. As he got out of bed, Ralph was surprised that his legs still felt like they had 25-pound weights on them. When he hit the floor, he almost fell.

"Do some stretching," said Fred. Ralph stretched a bit, and his legs did feel a little better.

"How am I going to ride a bike?" asked Ralph.

"Don't worry. It uses slightly different muscles, and it's not a difficult ride," answered Fred.

Ralph groaned as he put his pants on. "Those stairs are going to hurt!" said Ralph.

"You got this," said Fred.

"That phrase again – what does 'you got this' really mean?" thought Ralph.

Since Annie had to go to work, breakfast would be after the bike ride. Also, it was an excuse for skipping breakfast and working out first. Fred read that it was good to do that as part of a weight-loss routine. Ralph was, as always, looking forward to seeing Annie. When they met at the trail, they were both walking slowly. "Different leg muscles, says Fred," said Ralph.

"What?" replied Annie.

"Bike riding uses different leg muscles than running," said Ralph.

"Hmmm, I still have a feeling my legs are going to hurt when I ride the bike," said Annie.

"Of course, they will. I wonder if Fred doesn't sometimes make up crap just to get us to do something. Or maybe he is technically correct, but so what? Oh well, let's get this over with," said Ralph.

"I can hear you," said Fred.

"Good. Then stop making up crap," said Ralph.

"Just get on your bike," said Fred.

Ralph and Annie did some stretching but no jumping jacks. Ralph attempted to lift his leg over the center bike bar and failed. He had to lower his bike low enough so that he barely had to lift his leg. Annie's bike was more forgiving with the lower center bar, so she got on a bit easier.

After 45 minutes, it was time to stop. They had ridden enough, and Annie had to get to work. Annie remarked, "You know, I think my legs feel a bit better."

"Mine too, but let's wait and see," said Ralph. Later, after Annie was done working, they would go swimming.

After work, Annie met Ralph at the rec center for their swim. Annie and Ralph swam for half an hour – at a relaxed pace – and agreed it was dinnertime.

"Let's eat at my place tonight. I'm working on getting Wanda and Betty to eat our food. Everything they eat is so processed," said Annie.

"They do like some of my sauces. They'll come around, I think," said Ralph.

Ralph had a trick up his sleeve. He loved sauces, and he and Fred had been researching how to make a healthy yet tasty sauce that a teenager would like. "Sauce Is Boss is what I always say. I'm making a peanut sauce tonight," said Ralph.

"They do like peanuts. I think I'll tell them it's

unhealthy. Then they'll want to try it," said Annie.

"It is high in fat. Teenagers love fatty food. They won't know that peanut fat is healthier than bacon fat," said Fred.

Ralph stir-fried some veggies – broccoli, mushrooms, bell peppers, etc. He had some old boxes of brown sugar, flour, and white sugar that he set on the counter so that Wanda and Betty would think those ingredients would be in the sauce. Since they looked at their phones most of the time, it was easy to pretend to put them in the sauce when they were distracted.

"How will they ever drive a car?" he thought. Ralph made the peanut sauce along with some rice – "Teens gotta have carbs. Me too," thought Ralph.

It worked like a charm! "This isn't bad," said Wanda after a few bites.

"Are you sure you didn't get take-out?" said Betty.

"No. You can see all the boxes of the ingredients we used," said Annie. They finally noticed them.

After thoroughly enjoying the veggies, rice, and peanut sauce, Ralph said he had a surprise, "Cheesecake!".

Wanda and Betty almost fell out of their chairs. It never dawned on them that cheesecake could be relatively healthy, so there was no need to fool them. Plus, Ralph had made it at home, so they didn't need to see the ingredients. The secret ingredients were Greek yogurt and honey, so there was no refined sugar. He even added some oat fiber to the crust.

"Dinner wasn't bad at all," said Wanda.

"Coming from you, that's quite a compliment," said Annie. Wanda and Betty actually thought dinner was fantastic!

Wanda and Betty headed off to watch a movie, and Ralph said, "Thank you, Fred, for your research and step-by-step instructions, which made my job a lot easier."

"I'm glad Wanda and Betty had a healthy meal, albeit without knowing," said Annie.

Chapter 11

THE BIG PUSH

It had been three weeks now since Ralph and Annie had been training for the 10K. They stuck to the plan Fred set out "to a T." What's more, they were having a blast! The pain was gone, and running was getting easier. Ralph had lost 7 pounds now, and Annie 4. Today was going to be another test – 3½ miles. Never in their wildest (well, maybe their wildest) dreams did they ever think they could run 3½ miles! Still, 3½ is a way from 6.2 miles (10K).

Ralph and Annie met at the usual spot to do some stretching and jumping jacks. "We're running over half of the 10K mileage. Exciting!" said Ralph.

"It really is. And I feel great!" said Annie.

"Me too. Let's get the show on the road," said Ralph.

"Keep a study pace, and if you finish, I'll give you the winning lottery numbers before the drawing," said Fred.

"Can you do that? Why didn't you ever tell me?" said Ralph.

"Of course, I can't. Just run anyway," said Fred.

"He can be such an asshole," said Ralph to Annie.

The run was going great. After a couple of miles, it was time for a hill climb. "Race you to the top," said Annie and took off.

"I'm getting there first!" said Ralph.

Annie was surprisingly fast and had good stamina. But when Ralph put his mind to it, he was faster in the short run. Soon, he caught up to Annie and slightly passed her. They were both running as fast as they could. "I got you!" said Ralph. As he said that, he saw Annie disappear out of the corner of his eye. He then heard her hit the ground with a thud and begin screaming in pain.

"No! No!" yelled Ralph as he turned around. "Annie, please tell me you are OK. Please!" said Ralph as his heart pounded harder than ever.

"Aghhhhh! I'm not Ralph. I'm so sorry," said Annie.

"All that matters is that you're OK. Can you stand up?" asked Ralph.

Annie tried, but her ankle was too painful. "I can't, Ralph. It really hurts. Maybe it's broken or something. I think I stepped in a gopher hole," said Annie.

"Fred, do something! Can you?" said Ralph.

"My lack of human hands is a real problem here. But give me a second, and I'll guide you," said Fred.

"Hurry. I can't do this without Annie," said Ralph.

"You will do it with or without me. Do you understand? Do it **for** me!" said Annie.

"OK, OK. Come on, Fred. Tell me what to do!" said Ralph.

"Annie, did you feel or hear a snap?" asked Fred.

"I think so. But I was falling so I was worried about hitting my head. Maybe. I don't know for sure," said Annie.

"What do you think, sweetie?" said Ralph.

"I'm sorry. I just don't know," said Annie.

"Ralph, very gently rotate her ankle and tell me if either of you notices a grinding or crunching sound," said Fred.

Ralph does it. "Annie, do you hear or feel anything like grinding or crunching?" asked Ralph.

"It hurts so much. I just can't be sure. Maybe I need X-rays," said Annie.

"You definitely do. Nothing we do here will help you, so let's get to an emergency room," said Fred. "Ralph, if Annie puts her arm over your shoulders, can you help her keep her right foot off the ground?" said Fred.

"Yes. I'm a few inches taller, and she's pretty light," said Ralph.

"Thank you. Nice to hear I'm light," said Annie.

"OK. Let's go. It should take about 15 minutes to get to the car. Stop, Ralph, if you need to. Annie should put no weight on it," said Fred.

Off they went. They were making good time. "I need to stop for a minute. It really hurts," said Annie.

After a few minutes, they went again until they reached the car. Annie got settled in the back seat with her leg elevated. "Fred, direct me to the nearest emergency room. I can't think right now," said Ralph.

"OK. It's about 10 minutes – not bad," said Fred.

Upon arrival, Ralph helped Annie out, got her to the desk, and sat her down. "My guess from the way you walked in is that you hurt your leg," said Mary, the receptionist.

"No shit Sherlock," said Fred quietly.

"What was that?" said Mary.

"Nothing. I just said I'm glad we're here," said Ralph.

"OK. Take these forms and fill them out. A nurse will call you soon to take your vitals," said Mary.

"Thanks so much," said Annie.

They hobbled to a chair and completed the form. Soon, a nurse called Annie. They hobbled over to her. "My name is Jenny. Please have a seat," said the nurse.

After the vitals, Annie was given a wheelchair, and Ralph wheeled her to a room. After about 10 minutes, a man walked into the room. "I'm Dr. Robert. I understand you hurt your ankle running. Let's have a look," said Dr. Robert. He gently rotated Annie's ankle, but by now, it had swollen dramatically. After a few minutes, Dr. Robert said, "It's so swollen I can't be sure if it is a fracture or a sprain. You will need X-rays. I will order them. Wait about 5 minutes and head to the X-ray room."

The X-rays were taken, and Annie was told to go back to the room. Once there, Annie said, "Ralph, I mean it. Do not stop training just because I can't do it. In fact, I want you to train hard enough for both of us. Remember what it means to you and Joanie. If I can't run, I will still be there at the finish line cheering for both of you."

Ralph burst into tears. "I will, but it won't be the same. You don't understand how I feel when I see you at the trail in the mornings. I love you so much," he said.

"I love you too, and that's why I want you to do well in the 10K. I will be there for you in every way I can. Plus, you have Fred. Do you really think Fred will let you give up?" said Annie.

"OK. OK. You're right. I won't give up. Who knows what Fred would do? I will try harder than ever," said Ralph through his tears.

"That's my man. I have a feeling you are going to win that 10K or at least do yourself proud," said Annie.

Just then, Dr. Robert walked into the room. "I guess it's one of those good news/bad news situations. The good news is that it's not broken. The bad news is that it is a very bad sprain, and I recommend two weeks off it for a full recovery," said Dr. Robert.

"Oh no. Two weeks. That's a long time. Annie will lose all she gained or much of it," said Ralph.

"I'm already working on exercises she can do in the meantime," said Fred.

"Who said that?" said Dr. Robert as he looked around for another person.

"My watch. Fred is his name. He's been helping us train," said Ralph.

"Ah. One of those AI smart watches, huh? I've heard good things about them. No doubt Fred will keep Annie in shape while she mends. The main thing is to keep the strength and aerobics strong. Right Fred?" said Dr. Robert.

"Right, doctor. By the way, will you be giving Annie a boot to wear during recovery?" said Fred.

"Yes, Fred. I think it will be essential since you will be giving Annie an exercise program," said Dr. Robert.

"Thank you. No more questions," said Fred.

"Good luck to all of you. Nice to meet both of you. And you too, Fred. You're the first watch I've talked to. Good luck with the 10K. Be gentle with that ankle for a couple of weeks," said Dr. Robert.

"Nice to meet you as well, doctor. You're the first doctor I've talked to," said Fred.

Ralph took Annie home and got her settled on a couch. Ralph explained to Wanda and Betty that the three of them had to take care of Annie for a couple of weeks.

"Betty, you have food duty. Wanda, you get or bring your mom whatever she wants. I'll be happy to do whatever is needed when I'm here," said Ralph.

"OK. But who will drive us places?" said Wanda.

"I will. Just give me a schedule. I will work

around it. And, Annie, I promise I will follow Fred's training schedule. And you will be back on it too as soon as you are able," said Ralph.

"And I have a workout plan ready for Annie whenever she's ready. I've made sure that the ankle will be rested. Some of it involves upper body aerobics work in a pool, so Ralph get one of those boot waterproof covers from the pharmacy," said Fred.

"I promise to do my best," said Annie.

Ralph went to the store to get some groceries. Annie called Madge, the manager that works for her at the bakery.

"Madge, guess what? I sprained my ankle badly and will be off it for a couple of weeks. Can you take over? I'll be available to discuss things," said Annie.

"Oh no! How'd it happen? What about your training?" said Madge.

"I think I stepped in a gopher hole while Ralph and I ran. I went to the emergency room. It's not broken, but it really hurts a lot. I hope I'll be able to train for the 10K. I don't want to disappoint Ralph, but I can't put any weight on it," said Annie.

"You are one tough lady! I've known you for a long time. If anybody can do it – you can! And don't worry about the bakery. I'll run it just fine or hang myself," said Madge.

"I know you'll do a great job. And there'll be a bonus waiting for you when I'm better," said Annie.

"Take good care of yourself, and let me know if I can do anything at all for you," said Madge.

"Thanks. I have Ralph and the girls, so I'll be in good hands. Bye for now," said Annie.

"Bye, tough lady," said Madge.

Ralph returned with the groceries. Annie was sound asleep. Ralph needed a nap, so he took one on the reclining chair. At 7:00, he woke up. Annie was still sound asleep.

Ralph went to Wanda's room, where she and Betty were playing video games. "You two want something to eat? I have some of my special sauce left over – you guys loved it. I can put it over some pasta," said Ralph. He didn't mention he'd throw some veggies in.

"OK, I guess I would eat that," said Betty.

"I guess I will, too, but what about dessert?" said Wanda.

"Can't you girls skip dessert ever?" said Ralph.

"It's part of the meal – always," said Betty.

"All right, we'll figure something out," said Ralph.

After dinner, Ralph checked on Annie, and she was still sound asleep. "The painkillers really knocked her out," said Ralph. "OK, I'm going to sleep on the reclining chair in case your mom needs something. You two want to go watch a movie in Wanda's room?" said Ralph.

"OK," said Wanda. They went upstairs after grabbing a bag of popcorn from the pantry.

Ralph put on a movie and immediately fell asleep. Annie woke up early the next day and was surprised to see Ralph sleeping on the recliner. She grabbed her crutches and made her way to the bathroom. Ralph heard her and woke up. It took him several minutes to stand up straight. "My back is killing me," he said.

"I trust you can do your run and swim today. I'm giving Annie the day off but have her workout beginning tomorrow," said Fred.

"Are you sure she can do anything?" said Ralph.

"For the first few days, I have her doing seated and laying down exercises. Then, I add in some pool exercises. I think she'll be able to, but we'll see. I don't want her to fall too far behind," said Fred.

"I agree. I'll help her, of course. I really need her back beside me. I'm afraid she might give up trying to do the 10K. I have a big life-changing surprise planned for her at the finish line," said Ralph.

Ralph kept his word and did his training. Wanda and Betty helped Annie during those times. Annie had been doing her sitting and laying down exercises, but they were not as aerobic as she needed. It was time to get in the pool.

"You can do it, sweetheart. I know you feel pain, but you won't be putting weight on your ankle. The floatie around your waste will make it easy to keep your head out of the water," said Ralph.

"Use your upper body for now and work hard enough to get your heart rate up in the 150s," said Fred.

Ralph helped Annie into the pool. "It hurts a lot. Maybe I shouldn't do this. What if I make it worse?" said Annie.

"Fred, what do you think? Will this make it worse? Maybe she shouldn't do it?" said Ralph.

"Based on my review of the X-rays, I think she'll be fine. There will be pain, but it should subside over the coming week. Annie, if you don't do any exercise for two weeks, you will lose a lot of the muscle mass and stamina you were building. This way, we can keep it to a minimum," said Fred. Note to Ralph's file, "I hope I am doing the right thing. If Annie's injury worsens, she may be out of the 10K," wrote Fred.

"OK, OK. I will do what you tell me. I have faith in both of you," said Annie.

That night, Annie needed enough painkillers to bring the pain down to enable her to sleep. Ralph took his place on the recliner. He needed some painkillers for his aching back.

"Annie, thank you for trying. It means a lot to me. But if you can't do the training, just say so. I love you, and it won't matter a bit. I will continue working my ass off and make you and Joanie proud of me," said Ralph.

"I know. But I really was enjoying myself. So, I want to do it for you and me too. I can handle a lot of pain, so don't give up on me. Oh, and I love you too. Good night, and thank you for all you do for me," said Annie.

"Good night, my love," said Ralph.

For the next two weeks, Annie tried hard to follow Fred's routine. The pain did lessen each day, and the amount of weight she could put on it increased. Still, she was not able to put her full weight on the injured ankle without pain. So, she did what a tough lady would do. She hid the fact that she felt pain.

Ralph and Annie arrived at the trail at 9 a.m. "Today, you get to hike while I run further than I've ever run. Are you up for it? I'm not sure I am," said Ralph.

"Try to walk normally and let us know how you feel," said Fred.

Annie took several steps. She had not taken any painkillers that morning, so she would know how the healing was going. She felt a lot of pain. "Oh my. It does hurt, but I'll be fine. Go ahead and run, Ralph. I'm going to take my time. I'll be waiting when you're done," she said.

Annie walked, stopped, then walked some more for about 45 minutes. Then she waited on a bench at the spot where Ralph would finish. Soon, she saw him running towards her.

"Holy shit. He looks like he might pass out. She'd never seen him panting so hard. Ralph, you can do it. Just run to me," said Annie.

"I am," was all Ralph could get out. He finished and fell on the ground, panting.

"Your heart rate hit a new high —170. Does your family have any history of heart problems?" asked Fred.

"No. We always die of cancer," said Ralph.

"That's good to hear," said Fred.

"Kind of you to say that," said Ralph.

By now, Ralph could stand up and go to Annie. She hugged him. "You're my hero!" she said.

"And you're mine. How was your hike? Was there a lot of pain?" said Ralph.

"I did pretty well. I even got some cardio in going uphill. I hope I can do a lot more soon. You are way ahead of me now," said Annie.

"Well, tomorrow we see Dr. Robert. Hopefully, you can get back into some heavier training," said Ralph.

"You know his specialty is pediatrics. Not sure he is the one for ankle sprains," said Fred.

"Kids sprain their ankles all the time. It's not his first rodeo," said Ralph.

"Let's hope for the best," said Annie.

At 10 a.m. the following day, they saw Dr. Robert for a follow-up exam. "I'm going to rotate your ankle, and you tell me how much, if any, pain you feel," said Dr. Robert.

"I do feel pain, but it's not unbearable. In fact, it feels a lot better than just a few days ago," she said.

"The swelling seems to be gone. Must be that exercise program that Fred put you on. Fred, we may need you to train our physical therapists," said Dr. Robert.

"They can each get a watch just like me. That would give them someone knowledgeable to talk to," said Fred.

"Hmmm. We may want to investigate that.

Anyway, Annie, go on with your training. Listen to your body and take a break if your ankle insists, but I think you'll be fine," said Dr. Robert.

"Thank you so much. Hear that, Ralph. I'm coming after you! I'm going to train harder than ever. You will be eating my dust!" said Annie.

"That's what I like to hear. I'm so happy you're back," said Ralph.

Although it sounded like Annie was back, she was still only able to hike, albeit at an increasing pace. Annie was still feeling pain, but it was lessening, so that was encouraging. It had been over two weeks since she ran. Ralph was up to 3 miles. That night, they made a nice dinner – even the girls enjoyed it. The following morning, it was time to train. They met at the trail.

"So good to see you," said Ralph as he hugged her.

"So good to see you too," said Annie.

"I must admit my back feels better since not sleeping on your chair, but I did miss you. Fred, what is Annie doing today?" said Ralph.

"Well, Annie is going to hike a couple of miles with some slow runs up some hills. Make sure they are slow and stop if you feel a lot of pain. A little pain, I think, is OK. That's due to the stiffness. Before going, rotate your ankle and get it loose," said Fred.

"Got it. I seem to be able to put my full weight on the ankle and can walk fast, so I really think I can run in a few days," said Annie.

"So good to hear you say that. I was so worried that you wouldn't be able to do the 10K. If it weren't for Fred being on my ass every day, I doubt I would have kept the training up," said Ralph.

"You would have done it for Joanie," said Annie.

"Yeah, Fred kept reminding me of that," said Ralph.

"I'll meet you at the finish line. I'm going to run as much as I can," said Annie.

"OK. Be careful. No gopher holes," said Ralph as he watched Annie walk away, still limping a bit. "I don't think she'll ever be able to do a 10K," he said to himself.

Ralph did his run. He was up to 4 miles now. It was becoming more mental than physical as he got in better and better shape. He was stronger and lighter now but pacing himself was key. "How am I doing?" said Ralph.

"Heart rate is a little high, but that's because you're going slightly faster than usual," said Fred.

"I want to finish. Annie will be waiting," said Ralph through his panting.

"Agreed. But make sure you have some gas in the tank for the finish," said Fred.

"It's all mental now," said Ralph.

"Not all," said Fred.

Ralph finished in a personal best per mile. Annie was waiting with a hug. "Great run, Ralph. I'm going to have to get up to your speed. I did quite a bit of running today. I think I'm turning the corner," said Annie.

"I'm looking forward to having you right beside me," said Ralph.

"So, have you thought about dinner? I need to spend some time at the bakery. Madge has done such a great job it's almost like I'm not needed," said Annie. By now, Ralph and Annie had healthy dinner items they enjoyed making and some they enjoyed when eating out.

"Let's cook at home. Sauce is boss, and Fred has some new recipes. Madge has done a great job, but your customers really miss you. I saw the wall with all the get-well cards on it," said Ralph.

"Yeah, that is cool. Let's meet at my house around 6," said Annie.

"See you then," said Ralph.

As he walked to his car, Ralph asked Fred, "Am I on target for the 10K?"

"You have a way to go yet, but you can definitely do it," said Fred.

"What about Annie?" said Ralph.

"Hard to say. She will have to put in some hard training to get to the point you are at. It's possible, but only because she has the mental drive. Today, she was able to run a good deal, so it's time to get her back to running with you," said Fred.

"I like that," said Ralph.

"Try to run a bit slower until she gets up to speed. It may take a while," said Fred.

"Got it," said Ralph.

Ralph arrived at 6 p.m. Annie had texted that

she would be a little late. "Hi, Wanda. Want to help with dinner?" said Ralph.

"Sure. What can I do?" said Wanda.

"Cut up the veggies while Betty and I boil some water for the pasta," said Ralph.

Annie walked in about 10 minutes later. "I'm home. Wow, you guys are making some good progress," she said.

"Wait until you try this new sauce. I had to grind up pine nuts to make it. Very rich," said Ralph.

"It sure smells good," said Annie.

Dinner was ready, and they all sat down to eat. "This is your best sauce yet," said Wanda.

"Yeah, really good," said Betty.

"Ralph, you are the king of sauce!" said Annie.

"Thanks. You're going to need some calories because you'll be back to running with me tomorrow. Be sure to take it easy. I'll wait up for you," said Ralph.

"I'll do what I can," said Annie.

The morning arrived. "Do you think Annie can run? I'm worried," said Ralph.

"I guess we'll see," said Fred.

Annie and Ralph arrived at the trailhead. "OK, take it easy, sweetie," said Ralph.

"I'm actually feeling OK," said Annie.

They began running. Ralph was going slowly. Annie ran ahead.

"Hey, are you sure you can do this?" asked Ralph.

"Eat my dust," said Annie.

"What the? OK, I'm coming after you! Fred, what's going on?" said Ralph.

"It's amazing. I hope she can keep it up without hurting herself," said Fred.

Ralph caught up to Annie. "Are you sure about this?" said Ralph.

"I think the rest did me good. Plus, Fred's program kept me in decent shape. I feel great!" said Annie.

Ralph struggled but didn't want to let Annie know it. He tried not to pant, but it wasn't easy. Annie always seemed to have more stamina, but Ralph was shocked to be the one trying to keep up.

They finished the four miles side-by-side. "I can't believe what you just did!" said Ralph.

"I can't either. I think it's just mental," said Annie.

"I think Annie is a natural-born runner. Some people have more lung capacity than others. We can get back on schedule now," said Fred.

"Oh, Annie, you are more remarkable than I could imagine," said Ralph.

"I'm not about to let you run a 10K without me," said Annie.

The next morning, when Annie woke up, her legs were throbbing. Her lungs may have been able to handle the run, but her legs weren't ready. But her ankle was fine!

She texted Ralph, "Good news/ bad news. My ankle feels fine, but my leg muscles are killing me. Can barely walk. No run today. Swim? I do have to go to the bakery for a while."

Ralph got the text and said to Fred, "Annie can't walk. Her legs hurt too much. But her ankle doesn't hurt," said Ralph.

"Sounds good. Tell Annie to force herself to walk and stretch," said Fred.

Ralph texted Annie, "Fred says to walk and stretch. Try to keep loose. I'll see you at 6:00 for swimming. Love you!"

Annie texted back, "Will do. 6 p.m. it is. Love you too!"

Annie stretched her legs, and they did feel better. She clearly pushed herself too hard, but she made it! Her legs would heal, and her ankle was better. All in all, good news. She surprised herself with her ability to go the distance. "A natural born runner. I could've been in the Olympics. Maybe," she thought.

At 6 p.m., Ralph and Annie met for swimming. "The cool water feels good on my sore legs. I guess my lungs are fine, but my legs need some work. But I'm ready," said Annie.

"In my case, I think my lungs need work. I've never been great at long-distance running. I may need some lung work advice from Fred," said Ralph.

"Well, with the weight you lost and the strength you gained, you look great!" said Annie.

"You're biased. By the way, I've been downplaying the shape I'm getting in. I want to surprise Joanie big time! And you are in much better shape than me and look better than ever," said Ralph.

That night, when Ralph got home, he asked Fred, "How are we doing? Can we do the 10K? I feel so much stronger now, but we still have a way to go to run a 10K," said Ralph.

"Both of you are doing well. Annie's legs will be fine. We will be increasing the mileage fairly rapidly now. You and Annie really had no problem doing the 3½ miles, so we will do that again in a couple of days and then go to 4 miles next week. It sounds like a lot, but we are still a way from 6.2 miles. You have lost twelve pounds and gained a lot of strength. Over the next month, you should drop another five to eight pounds, and, with the strength and endurance gains, you will get to 5 to 5½ miles. That leaves a few weeks to get to 6 to 7 miles. I want you to go 7 miles because then 6.2 will be clearly within your range. I was originally thinking 10 miles, but 7 will do. I looked at the 10K route, and I don't see any major hills, so you and Annie will be fine," replied Fred.

"This is really exciting! I'm going to put on a hat and sunglasses and walk by Joanie when I see her. I bet she won't recognize my new physique. I want to thank you, Fred, for all your help. Wait, I guess that doesn't make sense. You are a watch just doing what you are programmed to do," said Ralph.

"Still, it is good to hear it. I am achieving what I have been programmed to do. You know, it is possible that one or both of us might win an AI Me award. The company gives awards to wearers who achieve goals that were set and accomplished with help from the watch. The wearer must have been wearing the watch regularly. With your weight drop and strength gain, together with finishing the 10K, you may have a chance. For me, I get no emotional satisfaction, but it does help AI Me in its marketing. They even do an awards online show," said Fred. Note to Ralph's file: cc Sam, "Ralph is exceeding expectations. All indications are that he now has a new lifestyle. Fred also wrote Sam separately, "Sam, have not heard from you in a while. Please contact me."

Five and a half more weeks of training to go. "My life has changed for the better so drastically in the last couple of months," thought Ralph. And it had. Annie came into his life. At first, they lived their old lives of eating unhealthy foods and getting little exercise despite Fred's coercion. Now, they welcome Fred's challenges and are getting better and better at accomplishing them.

Ralph gave Joanie a call. "Are you working out? Getting ready for the 10K?" asked Ralph.

"I am, but not as much as I'd like to. The kids keep me busy. How about you?" said Joanie.

"Doing okay. You know. Running some and working out some," said Ralph.

"Dad, you've never run a 10K before. You'd better work out hard. It's not easy. I don't want you to have a heart attack. Remember, I'm happy to be in the 10K with you whether you finish or not," said Joanie.

"OK, OK. I'll step it up. You're right," said Ralph.

Ralph loved keeping Joanie's expectations low.

He got off the phone and giggled like a little boy.

Ralph and Annie ran another 3½ mile run and now were moving up to 4 miles. They could tell that their endurance was increasing geometrically, if that's possible. An additional half mile didn't seem such a stretch when, not long ago, half a mile alone was difficult. "Ralph, you are on track. I heard what you said to Joanie. Don't worry. I won't spill the beans. She'll be surprised when you finish the 10K," said Fred.

Ralph loved hearing that. The light at the end of the tunnel was close, and it wasn't a train coming.

The following morning, Ralph and Annie met at the trail and did the usual stretching, jumping jacks, and high fives. This time, they each had a backpack with some water and a sports bar in it.

"How are your legs?" asked Ralph.

"Feeling much better," said Annie.

They took off. Ralph ran hard, but he was not able to put Annie away. She kept up with him, and they finished together.

"Hey, you're choosing to finish beside me. I mean —could you blow me away if you want to?" asked Ralph.

"No. I'm barely making it. I'm just keeping up with you," said Annie.

"It just seems you have more left in your tank than I have in mine," said Ralph.

"No way. I wish I did," said Annie.

Time for dinner. They both now lived new

lifestyles. The food also had become a habit at this point. Instead of craving fried food as they did at the beginning of the food changeover, they couldn't imagine eating it. Now, ice cream was a treat that still was worked into their regiment.

It was big push time! Ralph and Annie were now in the backstretch and heading towards the home stretch. In three days, they would run 5 miles. As with the 4-mile run, they knew they would be tired, but recovery would come sooner now. Their bodies had adapted to the impact of running, and their muscles could go the distance.

Ralph was 4 pounds away from his 10K goal of 178 pounds. Fred told Ralph, "You can eat a little more going forward. You are burning more and more calories."

"I'll eat to that!" said Ralph.

The 5-mile run went well. The last mile definitely strained both of them, but they knew what to expect. Ralph continued dropping weight and was now 2 pounds away from his goal, while Annie met her goal and could increase her calorie intake to maintain that weight.

It was now 3½ weeks before the "Joanie 10K," and it was time for their first practice 10K. "Am I ready for it?" asked Ralph.

"You keep asking me. Yes, you are ready for it. You are now at your weight goal, you have gained a substantial amount of strength, your lung capacity has increased dramatically, and you have a completely different mindset. You should feel more confident. Long-distance running is as much mental as physical," said Fred.

10K practice day arrived. Ralph and Annie were up having breakfast. Steel-cut oatmeal, fruit, and coffee were the choices for each of them. They were meeting at 7:30, so it was an early morning. "Today, we will do it! A full 10K," said Ralph when they met at the trail.

"I'm so proud of you," said Annie.

"I'm proud of us. Let's do this!" said Ralph. This was a day they thought would never arrive when they first started training. For them, they might have been training for the Olympics.

This was a big deal – to run a full 10K meant they could truly complete the Joanie 10K. Joanie would be so happy and proud of Ralph for making it. "But wait until she sees my new physique! Wow, she will be amazed!" thought Ralph.

The miles went by. Ralph and Annie were sweating. Ralph was worried he would not keep up. "Annie, I'm pushing myself hard," said Ralph.

"Fred, how is Ralph doing?" asked Annie.

"Could pass out at any moment. Just kidding. His heart is pounding but within an acceptable level," said Fred.

"You're a funny guy. Pass out, huh? You may end up in the electronics recycling bin," said Ralph.

"Just keep running. Remember, it's all mental now," said Fred.

They both finished together. Ralph tried to pull away, but he couldn't.

When they got home, Ralph said to Fred, "At the finish line of the Joanie 10K, there will be a large banner above the official finish line banner. It will say in large bold letters: "Annie, Will You Marry Me, Ralph?"

"Wow! Good for you! See, that shows confidence. If she says 'no,' you'll be fine," said Fred.

"I should know better than to talk to a robot. I won't be fine, you idiot! I'll be devastated, but it's worth the risk. Can't you see she means everything to me?" said Ralph.

"OK, OK, I get your point. And I'm not a robot. Anyway, my algorithms tell me that you two are a good match. And I do agree, it is worth the risk," said Fred. Note to Ralph's file cc. to Sam, "Ralph is going to ask Annie to marry him. I hope she says yes, but I worry that she is too independent to tie herself down again."

Time for 10K number 2. About a half mile from the finish, they looked at each other and picked up the pace. They still had some gas in the tank. "I'm finishing with a bang!" said Annie. In fact, they became a bit competitive, and the final ¼ mile turned into a race.

Ralph thought to himself, "I'll let her win. It'll make her feel good." At about the same time, Ralph was thinking that Annie turned on the burners and easily pulled away from Ralph. He gave it all he had, but it was hopeless. Ralph had to cough a bit because

Annie was kicking up some dust that flew in his face.

Annie hit the finish and yelled, "Yeah, baby!!" Ralph finished and wanted to believe he let her win, but he knew the truth – she beat him, and there was nothing he could have done.

Although Annie didn't gloat about winning, Ralph decided then and there that he had to work out harder before the Joanie 10K so he could beat Annie. Annie couldn't care less, but she did feel good about her performance. Luckily, Ralph kept his mouth shut except to tell Annie, "You ran a great race. Such a strong finish!" he said. Smart guy. Plus, he really was happy for Annie and proud of her. When he saw the proud look on her face, he couldn't help but give her a big congratulatory hug.

Ralph was now down to his 10K running weight, and it was 1½ weeks until the Joanie 10K. Time to do a 7-mile run. Once Ralph and Annie knew they could go further than a 10K with water on their backs, a 10K would be fairly easy.

Off they went. They always stayed together during most of the run. In the Joanie 10K, Ralph did want to do his best time to make Joanie proud. They finished the 7-mile run together and knew they were ready for the Joanie 10K.

Chapter 12

THE RACE IS ON

Time to fly to the Joanie 10K in Des Moines. Ralph had a plan for surprising Joanie. There was a "get-to-know-the-course" day the day before the race. Ralph told Joanie he would meet her there so he and Annie could get a feel for the course. Joanie had run this 10K before and knew the course, so she could explain it to her dad, and they could walk and jog some of it. Ralph had brought a tight tank top and shorts. He would walk by Joanie with a hat and sunglasses on and see if she recognized him. Hopefully, she would not. He was hoping to see the shock on her face when she realized it was him. He was in the best shape of his life and wanted to have some fun with it. Annie agreed to discreetly video Ralph's attempt to surprise Joanie.

Ralph got to the "get-to-know-the-course" day early so he could scope out the meeting place. Joanie suggested they meet near a burrito food truck that she liked. They served a veggie burrito that had real sautéed veggies (broccoli, mushrooms, bell peppers, etc.) with a sauce that she always ordered extra of. She figured her dad would want to head to a burger truck that was close by.

Ralph stood next to a tree where he could see the designated food truck, but it was shady, and he felt confident Joanie would not see him. Plus, there were a lot of people, so he was easily hidden. The key was for Ralph to keep an eye on Joanie and time his walk by without her noticing him. At least not noticing he was her dad. He did want her to notice him as an in-shape stranger. How would he make himself obvious to her without making it clear it was him? This was getting way more stressful than Ralph expected. If he walked by her in a crowd, then she would never notice him. If he walked by all by himself, then she might recognize him. Aha, he would ask another guy to walk by with him, and the other guy would be talking, but Ralph would be quiet, so Joanie didn't recognize his voice. He found his guy after a couple of interviews. His name was Bob. "Sounds like a fun idea," said Bob.

Ralph saw Joanie and said to Bob, "OK, it's time to roll. Just look at me and talk to me as we walk past the food truck. I will keep my eyes on you and not talk until we are well past it." Bob and Ralph did exactly what Ralph suggested. Bob's eyes were not what they used to be. He could see several people near the food truck, but it was too far away for him to recognize anyone. Ralph was careful to try and walk near enough to Joanie so she could get a good look at him but hopefully not recognize him. The plan was working perfectly. Joanie was standing there looking around for Ralph. Bob and Ralph were making their way toward the truck.

As Bob got closer, his eyes began to focus better. Annie was carefully videoing Bob and Ralph's saunter towards the food truck and was even able to pick some of Bob's voice. Once they were close enough for Bob to see the faces of people standing near the food truck, he saw a good friend of his. A person that he had run in some races with. "Joanie!" Bob called out. "I didn't think you would be here today since you've run this race several times before."

Ralph thought his plan was a big failure. Joanie would certainly recognize him now that Bob called her attention directly to them. "Bob, so good to see you! We are going to have nice weather for this event."

By now, Bob and Ralph were only about 10 feet away from Joanie. Bob assumed Ralph's daughter had never run in this race, so it never dawned on him that Joanie was Ralph's daughter. Ralph could tell that Joanie did not recognize him. His plan had worked! There he was. Right in front of his own daughter, and she did not know it was him!

"Joanie, this is a friend of mine," said Bob as he pointed to Ralph. Joanie stuck out her hand and smiled. Annie was getting it all on video. She couldn't believe that Ralph's plan had worked. She was so excited that she was shaking the camera a bit, but the camera had a "jiggle-proof" setting, so the video came out just fine. "This is Ralph," said Bob.

"Oh. My dad's name is Ralph," said Joanie as they shook hands. Joanie noticed a small scar on Ralph's right hand that he had gotten on a fishing trip they went on when she was 11. "What the....? Holy crap! Dad?" Joanie blurted out. She could not believe her eyes.

Ralph took off his hat and sunglasses and said, "Fooled you!"

"What happened to you? You're fit! Really fit! How did that happen? I mean, I guess I know how people get fit, but I never would have recognized you, and I mean that as a compliment."

Tears were now rolling down Joanie's cheeks. She was speechless, so she grabbed her dad, hugged him with all her might, and he did the same right back. "I'm so happy you did it," she cried.

"Me too," said Ralph. Bob was in shock. He never dreamed he would be part of such a beautiful moment. He teared up as well.

Annie was bawling at this point and had to stop videoing, but she had all the important parts. She slowly walked over but waited while Ralph and Joanie had their moment. For Joanie, it wasn't just that her dad was in better shape; it meant that he would likely live longer, and she would have more time with him, and maybe someday he would even become a great-grandfather. She stepped back and looked at him again. "I am just amazed!" she said.

Now Annie walked up. Joanie hadn't seen Annie before. "You two are made for each other! Both in great shape! That is fantastic!"

"We did it together. I could never have done it without her. And Fred," said Ralph.

"Fred? Oh yeah, that's right, Fred, the watch. I am so glad William and I got you, Fred. I want to hear the whole story, but I'm starving. I want to get something at this food truck, and then there is a burger truck over there for Dad," said Joanie.

"We want to eat at this one too. We're vegetarians now, and Annie is almost vegan. We love it! You have to try some of my homemade sauces. We put it over stir-fried veggies. I brought some. Annie has it in her purse. Try some on your burrito," said Ralph.

The tears rolled down Joanie's cheeks again. What a transformation! Last Christmas, she never would have dreamed that Fred would be so helpful. Of course, she realized that without Annie, Fred could not have done it alone. On top of it all, her dad looked the happiest she had ever seen him. And they were going to run in a 10K tomorrow together. She thought she would have to worry about him getting past the first mile. Now, it appeared he could finish. Maybe even beat her. Wait a minute. Beat her? That was a bit much. She felt some competitiveness well up inside of her but quickly suppressed it.

Time to eat. They each got a burrito and found a table. "Gimme some of that sauce, Dad. You say it's healthy? And tasty? I'll be the judge of that," said Joanie. Joanie put a little bit on her burrito and took a bite. "Fantastic! Just the right amount of spice and creaminess, and I also like the color too. Where did you get the recipe?" said Joanie.

"Fred," said Ralph.

"Fred? Are you kidding me? He does recipes?" said Joanie.

"Not only does he give me recipes, but Fred also watches while I make them and gives me step-by-step instructions. The whole time I am making it, Fred and I are talking and sometimes even making modifications based on my taste. Or Fred might even suggest an alteration based on the food the sauce will go on. It's incredible," replied Ralph.

"I had no idea that Fred could do so many things. And he helped you and Annie get in shape, too! Wow, what a great gift!" said Joanie.

"It really was. At first, I thought Fred was simply annoying, and sometimes he really was and still is (Ralph did not want to mention the shocking incidents, though). It got to the point that I couldn't go to the donut shop without getting into a big argument with Fred," said Ralph. Joanie laughed out loud.

"Why didn't you just take the watch off?" asked Joanie.

"It's not as easy as you think. Anyway, long story short, as time went by, I got to know Fred better and vice versa. Soon, we were watching sports and discussing players, stats, etc. We even watched the

World Cup, and now I understand soccer. It's like having a friend that knows everything there is to know. Plus, he has learned a lot about me. If I ask Fred to find me a restaurant, he knows exactly what Annie and I like to eat. If a light comes on in my car, I show it to Fred, and he tells me all about it and makes suggestions. He knows what movies I like and will find one for me. I could go on and on," explained Ralph.

"That is truly amazing! And you were so low-tech before," said Joanie.

"I still am. I just talk to Fred," said Ralph. Ralph went on to tell Joanie about his and Annie's physical transformations as well. The food part was easier. We actually liked the food from the start. And when we realized all the choices, and I started making sauces, the food part was a piece of cake – so to speak," said Ralph.

"I am simply flabbergasted. I never in my wildest dreams expected this, but I'm so happy for you, Dad. I am happy for all of us. It's a win all around. And thank you, Annie, for having arrived on the scene!" said Joanie.

"Oh, my pleasure. I can assure you. I am so glad I met Ralph! We are enjoying our lives together immensely! He is a hit with my daughters Wanda and Betty and even got them to eat healthier without them knowing it. Plus, he always has Fred with him, so if we ever need advice – it's like magic!" said Annie. Joanie had tears in her eyes again. So much good news!

"So, Dad, this new body you have – how do you feel? You look great. Are you always hungry? Tired? Is Fred working you too hard?" asked Joanie.

"I feel great! Fred is careful to push me just enough. Plus, the food is easy to digest. I am tired at the end of the day, so I sleep better. I drink very little alcohol and drink kombucha and green tea a lot. But the weird thing is that everything I do, eat, and drink now is because I enjoy it, so it is no longer a challenge. A beer does not tempt me. I still play poker sometimes, and I'll nurse a beer to keep from too much razzing from the guys. They're just jealous anyway. My transformation eats at them. No big deal. So, I am doing fine," said Ralph.

"OK, so now the big question. Are you going to beat me in the 10K? It sounds like you've been training way harder than me. Are you going to leave me in the dust? You look like you could do it," said Joanie.

"Well, of course, that doesn't matter at all. I will do my best, and that's all that matters. Three months ago, there was no way I would have finished. Now I know I will. That alone is a great feeling. Will I beat you? Hmmm. Maybe I will. But if I do, it will be because of you, Fred and Annie. And me – I suppose. But one thing is for certain. We will all celebrate no matter what the order of finish!" said Ralph.

It was getting late, and everyone needed a good night's sleep. It was a short walk back to the room, and Ralph told Annie to go ahead because he wanted to talk to Joanie about something. "Got a minute, Joanie?" said Ralph.

"Of course, Dad," said Joanie. "At the finish line, there will be a banner overhead. I wanted to tell you about it before you see it," said Ralph.

"What will it say? 'I WIN, DAD,'" said Joanie.

"No, it will say, 'WILL YOU MARRY ME ANNIE? RALPH,'" said Ralph.

"What?! Oh, Dad, I am so happy for you (tears again). That is wonderful! I Love Annie! But I don't think you need your name in the banner – she'll know," said Joanie.

"I suppose so. Oh well, too late. It's all set up," said Ralph.

Ralph went back to the room and wanted to tell Annie so badly what he had planned but did not want to spoil the surprise. Whenever he thought about the finish of the race with Annie seeing the banner, he would giggle like a 10-year-old – he seemed to be doing that more and more. Annie asked him, "Why are you giggling like a 10-year-old?"

Ralph just said, "I'm so excited about the race." And then it hit him. What if Annie says "no?" That had never dawned on him. Maybe she never wants to marry again. Maybe Betty and Wanda won't like the idea. Maybe, maybe... "Oh no, what am I doing?" thought Ralph. Plus, if Annie says "No" he'll be a fool in front of maybe a thousand people. Or what if she says "Yes" and then later tells him "No" to avoid embarrassment? What if, what if, ... ?

Ralph went into the bathroom and whispered to Fred, "What do you think will be Annie's answer?"

Fred said, "I don't have an algorithm for that situation – people are too unpredictable." Ralph didn't sleep as much as he would like. Annie slept like a rock but snored a lot. Maybe she slept more like a saw. Sawing logs all night.

Race day! Annie and Ralph got up, hugged, and could feel the adrenaline flowing. "Today's the day!" said Annie.

"I can't believe it's finally here! It is a day I will never forget. It is one of the three biggest days of my life!" said Ralph.

"Wow! I am honored to be a part of it!" said Annie. She didn't realize just how big of a role she would play but would soon find out when she got to the finish line. Ralph's heart was pumping hard.

"Relax," said Fred.

"There is no algorithm for my nervousness," said Ralph.

Fred replied, "You are right about that."

Ralph and Annie got on their running gear. It was a perfect day – sunny with a high of 75. Could not be better. Breakfast time.

Joanie had a hard time sleeping. She was so happy and excited for her dad. Plus, she couldn't get over the shape he got into. She was simply too happy to sleep a lot. But, like Ralph and Annie, she had plenty of adrenaline flowing, so she would have no problem with the run. Plus, she ran races longer than 10K – she'd even completed two marathons – so a 10K would just be a warmup. Oh yeah, the finish line. The finish line! That's when Annie and her dad get engaged – fantastic! It never dawned on Joanie that Annie might say "No." Luckily, Joanie could run her race without the worries Ralph had regarding Annie's answer.

The three of them got together for breakfast. They all had oatmeal, fruit, and coffee. Ralph likes nuts in his oatmeal, so he piled some on. Annie and Joanie had some as well. They finished it off with a glass of water for hydration. It was about an hour before the race started, so they headed over to the starting area. Ralph was surprised to see so many people. "How can this many people run so far?" he thought. To Ralph, a 10K was a long distance. To most people in the total population, it really was too, but to most people in the race, it wasn't. As it got closer to race time (8 a.m.), the runners congregated around the starting line. Each runner was given a sensor to wear, so it did not matter whether a person started before another person. The sensor would not start until a person crossed the starting line. Then, when the person crossed the finish line, the sensor would record the runner's time. Ralph was sweating, thinking about the finish line with the banner overhead. What had he done? He must be crazy, he thought.

It was 7:59 a.m. Ralph, Annie, and Joanie looked at each other. "Here we go," said Ralph.

At 8 a.m. am sharp, the announcer said, "Go!" and in a fairly orderly fashion, the runners began running. Ralph, Annie, and Joanie were side-by-side as they began. They stayed that way for quite a while. Each one wondered how the race would play out. Joanie was thinking she could probably take off and leave them in the dust even with her dad's much better condition. Ralph thought maybe he could beat Joanie, but he wanted to cross at the same time as Annie so he could learn his fate immediately. Annie was thinking about how fun it was to be there and could not care less about how well she did as long as she finished.

At the 3-mile mark, they were all still together and even able to keep talking to each other. "You and Annie are in such great shape!" said Joanie.

There was a time not too long ago when Ralph would have either been panting by now or quit a long time ago. But here he was. Talking and enjoying the run. "Thanks, Joanie, and thanks for letting us keep up with you," said Ralph.

"You think I'm letting you? No, I'm pushing myself," said Joanie. Her strained smile faded a little further when she heard Fred declaring to Ralph, "You the Man!" as further encouragement.

At the 4-mile mark, all three were still running together. Joanie now knew for sure that her dad and Annie really were ready for a 10K. Joanie sped up a little but was surprised to see them catch up so easily.

At the 5-mile mark, they were all running

together at Joanie's faster pace. During the last quarter mile of mile 5, Joanie kicked it up a notch. Ralph and Annie realized immediately that they hadn't slowed down, but that Joanie had turned this into a race. Ralph and Annie quickly caught up to Joanie and were stride for stride again. Joanie was shocked. Was this the same Dad who couldn't keep up with her on short walks five months ago? The same Dad that carried a lot of belly fat around? The same Dad that stopped halfway up the stairs to catch his breath?

At the 6-mile mark, Joanie had not shaken Ralph and Annie. "Joanie, are you going to speed up again? I'm running out of gears," said Ralph.

"I'm going about as fast as I can. You two are impressive!" said Joanie.

"I'm just glad to be here," said Annie.

"Here, here!" said Ralph.

"All present, all correct," chimed in Fred.

They were all now breathing hard and could feel the strain but knew the race was almost over. It was now or never. Joanie gave it all she had. Ralph and Annie were ready, and all put their heads down and ran as fast as they could. Joanie got a couple of strides ahead, but Ralph and Annie closed it again. As the finish line drew nearer, Joanie realized that any one of them could win. What a surprise! She would have bet this type of finish was simply never going to happen. Maybe she should have trained harder, but she saw no need. With only 50 yards to go, Joanie was able to gain a stride on them. When they crossed the finish line, Joanie was one stride ahead, and Ralph and Annie ended in a dead heat. They tied. They all ran through the finish line and were 30 yards past it with their heads down, panting.

Ralph hugged Annie and Joanie and said, "I am the happiest man in the world! I just finished a race with two women I am madly in love with!" Then it hit him. None of them had noticed the banner over the finish line. Ralph had to think of a reason for all of them to go back in front of the finish line. Was the banner there? He had no idea. All three were looking down when crossing. Now came a moment much bigger than the race. Annie had to see the banner. "I think I dropped the room key just before the finish line," said Ralph.

"Don't worry, sweetie, I have one in my purse in the car," said Annie.

How was Ralph going to get Annie back in front of the finish line to see the banner, and was the banner even there? Maybe it wasn't there, but he was so focused on the race he couldn't be sure. He needed Joanie's help. She had forgotten about the banner too. Ralph hugged Joanie again and said, "Annie didn't see the banner."

"Neither did I. Was it there?" said Joanie.

"I don't know, but we have to get Annie back there to see it," said Ralph. Joanie and Ralph parted and looked at each other.

"Right. Uh. Annie, there is something I noticed

at the finish line that I wanted you to see since you've never run the race here before," said Joanie.

"OK, sure," said Annie.

"Good job!" whispered Ralph in Joanie's ear.

They turned to walk back to in front of the finish line. They had to walk outside the course since many runners were still crossing the line. As Ralph walked, he thought, "So this is it. I just finished a race with the two women I love – my daughter and maybe my fiancé. Now we are walking to see if Annie will truly become my fiancé." Ralph's life had changed in many ways over the past few months, but he was about to find out if it would have an even bigger change right now. They made their way through the crowd and arrived in front of the finish line. Ralph looked above the finish line, and there it was. A banner reading in bold letters, "WILL YOU MARRY ME ANNIE? RALPH". Annie was looking around, wondering what Joanie wanted her to see.

Joanie directed Annie's attention to the banner above the finish line. It was red letters on a white background, and the print was so large that a person would have to be legally blind not to be able to read it. Numerous people were also looking at it, wondering who Ralph and Annie were. Annie looked up, and she at first wondered who they were as well. Then it dawned on her like a ton of bricks. Annie covered her face with her hands. Maybe because of the energy expended in the race and the need for fluids, Annie felt lightheaded. In fact, Annie was suddenly unable to focus and, before long, began to fall backward. Luckily Ralph was nearby and caught her as she fell.

By the time Annie reached the ground, she was unconscious. "Give her some space!" yelled Ralph.

"Does anybody have some water?" yelled Joanie. Right about then, a volunteer from the race came up with some water. After about 15 seconds, Annie opened her eyes. Ralph said, "Can you sit up?"

"What's her name?" asked the volunteer.

"Annie," said Joanie.

"That's the same name as on the banner," pointed out the volunteer.

"We know," said Joanie.

"Are you OK?" said Ralph. He had tears in his eyes and felt awful because Annie's reaction to seeing the banner could not have been more opposite to what he wanted. He was planning to return the engagement ring. His dreams were shattered. What had been a wonderful day was turning out to be one of his worst. And Annie might be injured. He luckily caught her, or she would have hit her head and maybe had a concussion. All that mattered at this moment was that Annie was not hurt. "Can you sit up?" said Ralph.

Annie whispered, "Yes," but made no attempt to sit up.

Ralph was worried. Annie said she could sit up but made no attempt. Annie said louder, "Yes."

"Well then, sit up, my dear," said Ralph. He

was crying now because it appeared Annie had lost control of her body and may be paralyzed. And it was his fault. He was getting sick to his stomach. "Somebody call an ambulance!" yelled Ralph.

Fred piped up, calculating frantically, "Let me handle this, just assessing the best service to call!"

It was then Annie realized Ralph had not understood what she was saying "Yes" to. Annie jumped up and said, "Do not call an ambulance! What I need is an engagement ring from this man!"

Ralph's tears went from sadness to joy in a flash. The crowd cheered! "She said yes! I am so lucky! I am so happy!" said Ralph.

We are both so happy!" yelled Annie.

"Me too!" added Joanie. Time for a group hug! The three of them hugged while the crowd cheered. Of course, there were several videos taken, so Ralph and Annie had the opportunity to see their engagement from several angles afterward.

Ralph pinched himself hard enough for it to hurt. It hurt. He wasn't dreaming. The three of them needed some fluids badly, so they headed to get their backpacks. Ralph said to Fred, "Can you believe it? I don't deserve to be so happy. But I am, and a lot of it is thanks to you. Annie and I have found things we would never have enjoyed if you hadn't forced us."

"I simply had a priority of helping you meet your goals. I did what was logical to hopefully get you there. You did the rest. Although I am not programmed to feel happy, I sense something I'm not sure how to describe. I do fully understand that you achieved your goals in a big way, and I will bring it to the attention of AI Me. Maybe we'll get an award," said Fred.

"That would be cool," said Ralph.

"I'm going to call the girls to give them the good news –finished the race and getting married," said Annie. She hoped they would be excited by both. So did Ralph.

"I am stunned," said Joanie.

"Yes, our engagement is fantastic!" said Ralph.

"No, stunned that you two kept up with me. I've run a lot of 10Ks, and this is your first. And five months ago, Dad, you had trouble making it all the way across the street. Well, not that bad, but you know what I mean. You two ran like track stars, especially for your age. Wait a minute, I didn't mean to say that either. I'm just so stunned!" said Joanie.

"Well, I'm glad you are stunned in a good way!" said Ralph

"Absolutely," said Joanie.

Annie reached Wanda and Betty, "Guess what? We finished the race! Isn't that exciting?" said Annie.

"Fantastic mom. When are you coming home? We like Madge but need some tasty food," said Wanda.

"I have more news. Ralph and I are getting married," said Annie. There was silence so she repeated herself.

"Are you sure?" said Betty.

"Yes, sweety. Isn't that exciting?" said Annie.

"I guess so. We do like Ralph and his sauces. Yeah, that's cool," said Wanda.

"Cool," said Betty.

"OK. Cool. Bye. I love you," said Annie. Annie returned to Ralph and Joanie.

'What did they say?" said Ralph.

"They are very happy about it," said Annie.

"That's fantastic!" said Ralph.

"I'm so glad," said Joanie.

"Well, time to get cleaned up. What about an early dinner?" said Ralph.

"Of course. Where would you like to go?" said Joanie.

"Just pick one of those healthy restaurants you always tried to drag me to," said Ralph.

They got back to the room. Annie got in the shower first. Ralph just wanted to lay on the bed and stare at the ceiling. He was now engaged to a woman he was madly in love with. Life takes its twists and turns, and now, it has turned in the right direction. He took a deep breath and drank it all in. The important thing in life is to appreciate the good times because the bad times will come without a warning, he thought. He heard Annie gently singing in the shower. Although the shower sound muddled it, and she wasn't singing loudly, it was the most beautiful song he had ever heard. Soon he and Annie would be planning their wedding. How cool is that? "Very cool," he said.

"Temperature 73 degrees," said Fred.

"No, you crazy gizmo, my life is very cool. In fact, it's perfect! I did a 10K with Joanie, I'm engaged to Annie, you're not as much of a pain in the ass as you used to be. I just want to cherish the moment."

"I'm not a gizmo nor a pain in the ass, but I get your awkward human humor. Also, I do agree that you are riding a perfect wave of life. I, of course, take credit for your physical achievements, but you can take at least some of the credit for wooing Annie," said Fred.

"I'll ignore your awkward gizmo humor. And I take full credit for Annie. Well, most of the credit. Your recipes helped a little. Anyway, I'm just saying I'm happy!" said Ralph.

"I get it. Sincerely, you earned it and have a right to dwell on the moment. I'm happy for you," said Fred.

"Thanks, Fred. You really are OK – for a gizmo," said Ralph.

"And you're OK for a human," said Fred.

Joanie came out, and Ralph went in the shower. He was careful not to sing. Carrying a tune was something foreign to him.

They were cleaned up and starving. "Should I bring the sauce?" asked Ralph.

"Yes. It makes everything taste better!" said Annie.

"Good point! No matter what we get, we can add some sauce," said Ralph.

"Except dessert," said Annie.

"Right. Need to work on dessert sauces," said Ralph as they seemed to float down the stairs without touching them. They both wondered before the race how they would feel after – leg pain, cramps, blisters, etc. Instead of blisters, they just felt bliss.

Sprout My Grains was the name of the restaurant Joanie selected. What a night! So many reasons to celebrate: Finishing the race, running well, engagement, being alive, and being with people you love. Joanie was careful to focus on Annie and Ralph's engagement and how well they did in the 10K. She didn't mention who was first among them. She did vow to herself to train harder, though. "So, what do you two like to eat most?" asked Joanie.

"Well, I am a vegetarian, not a vegan, so I do like something with some cheese in it. I used to want it to be 90% cheese. Now I can accept less than half (with a smile on his face). So, vegetarian lasagna is maybe my favorite, various pizzas are good, veggie bowls with my sauce are great, vegetarian burritos with some cheese in them are good, quiche... anyway, I like lots of stuff," said Ralph.

"Don't get him started on desserts. Assume if it's dessert, he likes it. (Ralph smiled in agreement) I try to be vegan, although occasionally, I fall off the wagon. I like pretty much the same as Ralph, except I will go for no cheese or eggs or maybe a little. Now vegan cheese, I will load up on," said Annie.

"Good. I think we all like the same foods. We can go to the same restaurants now without someone having to search the menu for something to eat," said Joanie.

"So, Dad, tell me more about Fred and how he

got you so fit. I may be getting one myself. You must have trained hard! You and Annie's transformations are remarkable!" said Joanie.

"I think first I had to know and understand that Fred had my best interest in mind. And it had to match my personal interest. When I realized that, I put myself in his hands. So, that's it, really," said Ralph.

"So, I guess the watch only works if the wearer and watch goals match. Although, if you told me when you got the watch that your goals were to be in the shape you are now in, I would have told you to set your sights lower," said Joanie.

"Thank you, Joanie. It means a lot hearing that from you. You've always been in great shape. You and I disagreed on eating and working out previously, but I always knew you were right," said Ralph.

"Me too. I ate lots of unhealthy stuff and never worked out except for a walk or an easy bike ride. Ralph and Fred have been my guides and my trainers. I am lucky," said Annie.

After the meal and talking a lot, everyone was exhausted. Ralph and Annie were spending a couple more days in town with Joanie, so they would have plenty of time to catch up and celebrate the engagement. Tomorrow would be a relaxing day. A walk around Des Moines East Village was planned, but mainly to enjoy the coffee shops and cafes. Ralph was curious as to whether he would be sore, so he asked Fred about it.

Fred said, "You did push yourself harder than ever today, so expect some stiffness. Tomorrow, do some stretching."

Annie and Ralph got in bed exhausted, and in no time, they were both sound asleep with smiles on their faces.

Morning arrived soon, and Ralph's alarm (i.e., Fred) went off. Fred chose to play some relaxing music that gradually got louder. He chose the "Blue Danube Waltz" by Strauss. Ralph thought he was dreaming. He still was – about the finish line and how they missed seeing the banner – and then the music gently worked its way in. Then he remembered he and Annie were engaged, and his heart started pumping. Soon he was up and woke Annie as he got out of bed. "Good morning, my bride-to-be," said Ralph.

"Good morning, my husband-to-be," said Annie as she got out of bed for a hug.

"Stretching and a relaxing walk are what we need today, says Fred," said Ralph.

"I never disagree with Fred," said Annie.

Joanie awoke and noticed quite a bit of stiffness. She did not expect to run hard yesterday, so she pushed herself beyond what she was ready for. She got out of bed and walked slowly towards the bathroom. "Hmmm. We may have to do a short walk today," she said to herself. Joanie assumed her dad and Annie would be in even more pain than she was, so they would not want to do much walking either.

Yes, assumptions can make an ass out of you and me. When Joanie met up with Ralph and Annie, they were ready to see the town and some trails through the park. "You're kidding me. You two are feeling fine?" said Joanie.

"Not bad. A bit stiff, but we did some stretching. We are probably stiffer than you, so please go slowly," said Ralph.

"Oh, OK. Yeah, I'll slow down my pace. No doubt the two of you are sore. But we can have some coffee and breakfast first," said Joanie.

"Let's go to the Coffee Grinder. I read it's got great coffee. Annie and I might split a pastry. It's about a 15-minute walk only," said Ralph.

"Yeah, 15-minute walk. Sure. We can go there. It is good. I go there often," said Joanie. As they walked off, Joanie did her best not to show the pain she was in. She avoided painkillers whenever possible, but this might be the time for them. They walked for about 5 minutes.

"You don't have to go that slowly, Joanie. But we do appreciate it. Maybe you feel guilty for beating us," Ralph said.

"I don't mind. I want the two of you to enjoy a leisurely morning stroll and enjoy the Old Town. A lot of remodeling has been done. Aren't the buildings beautiful?" said Joanie as she grimaced.

"They really are. I am enjoying our stroll, but I do look forward to some good coffee," said Annie.

As they turned a corner, Ralph saw the Coffee

Grinder sign. "Finally. I mean, I need some coffee," said Joanie.

"Me too," said Ralph and Annie in unison.

"That was such a nice stroll. Thank you again for going slowly, Joanie. Wow, look at those pastries!" said Ralph.

"What's nice about this place is they have a great selection of healthy pastries – no added sugar, whole grains, and gluten-free and dairy-free if you like. The sweetness comes from pieces of fruit in the pastries. Oat milk is used wherever possible. Annie, you probably know all about this kind of stuff," said Joanie.

"This is very exciting for me. I am getting lots of ideas, and I may even want to speak with the owner," said Annie.

"Well, my stomach has lots of ideas. I may get one of each," said Ralph. One of the benefits of eating healthy for Ralph was that he could really fill up.

They each ordered a fair amount of items and planned to share "family-style." Ralph knew he would get the largest portions. "We're going to need to do some decent walking to burn off these calories," said Ralph.

"Maybe just don't eat too much," said Joanie.

"Oh Joanie, one thing I haven't lost is my appetite. Don't worry, Annie and I will do our best to pick up the pace so we can be hungry for lunch," said Ralph.

"You two are amazing," said Joanie.

"Thank you, sweetie. I couldn't wait to show

you the new me," said Ralph. Joanie truly was happy to see her dad's new physical condition, but for the moment, she regretted it.

"So, Joanie, maybe we should do another run," said Ralph.

Joanie just about spit her coffee out. "Today?" she said, somewhat in a state of panic.

"No way. You could, but we couldn't. I mean in 2 or 3 months. In another town so we can explore a place neither of us has been to," said Ralph.

"Yes. Absolutely. That would be a blast! (And it would give Joanie time to train more). Have you two ever considered running a half marathon?" asked Joanie.

"Whoa. That's like twice as long as a 10K. I don't know if we could ever do that. I would have to discuss it with Fred," said Ralph.

"I saw the two of you run yesterday. You can do it. It's simply a matter of training. A half marathon is a bit more mental because it takes a lot longer, but if you train for it, no big deal," said Joanie.

"OK. No promises, but we will think about it. Let's go walk around some more," said Ralph.

It was a lovely day for walking, enjoying the sights, eating and then they were going to a concert in the park. After the concert, all of them were looking forward to some sleep. Ralph and Annie headed back to their room.

They were truly enjoying the moment. Engaged! How about that! Neither of them could have wished for anything more. On top of that, they were living a great life with so much in common. "A half marathon? Do you think we could do it?" said Ralph.

"I don't know. Twice as far as we just ran? That's a long way. We'll have to give it some thought. I would want to know what Fred thinks, too. For now, let's just enjoy our success," said Annie.

Morning came, and Joanie felt lots better. Annie and Ralph slept well and were ready for coffee and more exploring. The coffee place yesterday was so good they went there again. The Des Moines River went through town, so they decided to hike on a path alongside it and see how far they could get.

As they finished lunch, they enjoyed seeing the river go by. There were some kayakers and paddleboarders gliding along. "I would like to try that. I've never paddleboarded," said Ralph.

"In your new shape, you wouldn't have any trouble. Neither would Annie. You really don't have to be in good shape, but it helps. I think a person's balance is better. We can give it a try tomorrow morning. There is a paddleboard rental place in town," said Joanie. Ralph and Annie had one more day there. Luckily that would be the last day before a storm moved in. After a quick dinner at the food trucks, it was time for some sleep.

"Paddleboarding tomorrow. You think it will be hard?" asked Ralph.

"I see people doing it all the time. Very popular nowadays. I'm sure we'll suck at it, but if we like it, we can do it more and get better," said Annie.

"I wonder if Fred can help us. Probably not. We might be on our own this time. Fred, can you teach us how to paddleboard in 10 minutes or less?" asked Ralph.

"I'm a watch, not a magician. But, still, I can't do much but show you some videos of people taking lessons," said Fred. So, Ralph and Annie sat and watched videos on Ralph's computer of people learning to paddleboard.

Another beautiful morning. But it was a red sky. "Isn't a red sky in the morning a sailor's warning?" asked Ralph.

"I believe you are correct. Not sure why. But I've heard that a storm is coming," said Annie.

"Well, hopefully, it will hold off until we are gone tonight. In the meantime, let's have another great day. We can put those paddleboarding lessons to good use," said Ralph.

"Don't count on that (Annie said, laughing). If I can stand up at all, I'll be happy. Hopefully, we can enjoy it enough to try and get better in the future. I've seen people do it, and they look like they're having fun," said Annie.

Joanie was already up and had made a reservation at the paddleboarding shop called "Paddle Me." Two beginners and one intermediate. Joanie was decent but no expert. She had no problem navigating Saylorville Lake on a calm day, and it was calm now. She picked up her dad and Annie. They all had some breakfast and headed to the lake – about a 30-minute drive. "Another beautiful morning," said Joanie.

"I did see a red sky this morning," said Ralph.

"What's that mean?" asked Joanie.

"I think a chance of rain later in the day," said Ralph.

"My phone does show rain later today, but we'll be done by then," said Joanie.

"Glad to hear that," said Annie.

At Paddle Me, they filled out the paperwork saying that if they die paddleboarding, it's their own fault, even if the paddleboard explodes and sends them onto the rocks, crushing their skulls. Nobody ever reads the fine print.

Joanie had her own paddleboard – a blow-up one that was fine for a calm lake. Ralph and Annie rented solid boards. The instructor gave them some tips – "Stand up and paddle while not falling off. If you fall off, climb back on carefully without tipping the board," the instructor said.

"Great advice," said Ralph.

"Don't forget," said Annie.

Off they went. Soon, Ralph had a mouthful of lake water after a summersault into the water. "Great form!" said Annie.

"That looked like fun!" said Joanie.

"Wow! Good thing I hit the water feet first! Now I understand why we signed those waivers! But I'm OK. Now, I will gently and carefully crawl back on the board," said Ralph. Two summersaults later,

Ralph was back on his board. He thought he heard Fred laugh, but Fred would not admit to it. "All right, all right – enough messing around," said Ralph. He looked over and saw Joanie calmly paddling around him – waiting and saying something he could not hear. Annie was doing well – staying upright, but her lack of movement meant she could be mistaken for a statue.

"Keep your feet wider and shift your weight only slightly when you paddle. And paddle smoothly. Let the paddle glide through the water. Don't pull too hard," said Fred.

"Now, you tell me," said Ralph.

"It was all in the videos last night," said Fred. Ralph was able to climb back on the board and stand by keeping his feet a little wider. He and Annie looked quite similar, standing on their boards, petrified of too much movement.

"Relax. I know it's not easy the first time, but it's kinda like dancing. You have to feel the movement of your partner and work together," said Joanie.

"Great. You know how good I am at dancing," said Ralph.

"You've gotten a lot better, sweetie," said Annie.

After an hour, they saw a place to go ashore and take a break. Terra firma felt great to Ralph and Annie. They were happy with their progress. Ralph was able to look down on the water now instead of up through it. Much more fun. "Remember that red sky this morning?" said Ralph.

"Sure do," said Annie.

"Well, it seems it's gotten cloudy, and a breeze is picking up. Fred, what do you see for the weather here?" asked Ralph.

"The cold front seems to be moving in a little quicker than expected this morning. The winds could pick up to around ten mph in the next hour. Of course, weather is unpredictable," said Fred.

"No kidding, Sherlock. I thought you knew everything," said Ralph.

"Not the future," said Fred.

"We'd better wrap it up here and head back. One thing you don't want when you are learning to paddleboard is a lot of wind and waves," said Joanie.

"It's not too bad yet," said Ralph.

"Getting a little choppy," said Annie. It soon got a lot choppier and windier. Ralph had perfected his summersaults off the board and got to do a couple more for everyone's entertainment. Annie was sitting on her board and getting very cold. Joanie had called the paddleboard office, and a boat was on its way.

"Let's just sit here and wait for the boat. I can't go anywhere," said Ralph.

Soon, they were in the boat together with their boards and headed back. "I had fun. Even though it ended a bit crazy," said Annie.

"Me too. I never realized I could do summersaults so well," said Ralph.

"Well, Dad, I'm impressed! I would have broken my neck in 20 different places if I had done the summersaults you did! That was amazing! Where did you ever learn to do that?" asked Joanie.

"I wouldn't say I learned to do summersaults off a paddleboard, but we did lots of tumbling when I played football in high school. What I did learn was to keep going over. Don't stop or you will land on your head – not good," said Ralph.

When they reached the shore, the wind was strong, and it was starting to rain. They got there just in time.

By the time they finished dinner and Joanie was taking them to the airport, the storm was in full force. Ralph asked Fred, "Is the plane on time?"

Fred said, "Yes, so far." When they arrived, they said a quick goodbye since all three were getting soaked, and Ralph and Annie ran into the airport. They checked in. They both had only carry-on bags, so it went quickly. The flight was bumpy. Especially the take-off. Nobody stood up during the flight much. But they made it and landed safely. It was calmer on the landing end, so that was nice.

Ralph's car was in the airport parking lot, so they made their way to it. "You know, we should go somewhere off the beaten path and relax. Maybe a cabin in the woods. Up in the mountains. Get away from it all," said Ralph.

"That sounds like a great idea. I am busy with the bakery during the summer. How about at the end? Also, we must plan the wedding. Maybe a wedding at the end of summer and a honeymoon at the cabin," said Annie.

"That's perfect! In the meantime, we can keep training like we have been. I'm not sure about a half marathon, but I'm not ruling it out," said Ralph.

When they got in the car and started to leave the airport, Ralph turned on the radio. A song called "Goin' To Montana" came on, and they listened and looked at each other. "Montana," they said at the same time. They sang along, "Honey, let's go explore." So, that was set. Wedding at the end of summer with a honeymoon at a cabin in the mountains of Montana. Life can be a dream... life can be a dream...

"Ralph, what do you have in mind for the wedding? The weather should be nice so something outside would be good. I'm thinking of a small wedding. How about the backyard? We could put a lot of flowers around. And we would save money!" said Annie.

"You are right. That's what I was thinking. Instead of spending money on a big wedding, we can maybe use it for a vacation next year. Maybe even do a run in Paris or something with Joanie. How cool would that be?" said Ralph.

"As cool as a winter's night in Fairbanks!" said Annie.

"It's a deal then. Let's look at the calendar," said Ralph. He suggested September 29th, a Sunday.

'That's not such a great time for the bakery. I promised a friend from way back I'd cover her 40th birthday party catering," said Annie. Ralph frowned.

"I don't want to go to a wedding any time. They take so long," said Wanda, as she and Betty vacated the room in search of other entertainment.

Ralph nervously glanced at Fred looking for help, who stayed silent figuring he had not

enough data available for advising on this very human situation. Ralph desperately wanted the whole family to be together at the wedding but felt he could not get heavy with the girls or Annie and try to insist they all agree a date. "This could get awkward," he thought.

Then, a few seconds later, Annie said with a smile, "August 29th though, would be fine.

The girls don't start school until mid-September, so we should just bring it forward some more – no time like the near future."

Anxious at another change in direction and not wanting to displease anyone, Ralph asked, "What about Wanda... the girls... ?"

"The girls don't get a choice. This is important to me. So they are going and it will be great," said Annie firmly. And that was that.

Although Annie was truly excited about the wedding, she had spent some very hard years building the business and was now reaping the rewards. Plus, she liked it! The loyal customers were so fun to see each day. It kept her busy. And it was special to see Ralph because she would miss him while at work. "It's a big decision. But I do agree it would be fun to travel all over the world. We're not getting any younger, and I would like to see as much of it as I can. I love you, Ralph. I would never do it if it weren't for that," said Annie.

"I love you too and will love you either way. I mean that. Do not sell your business unless you want to. We will travel as much as we can, and one day of travel with you is worth a year of traveling without you," said Ralph as he hugged Annie tightly.

"Just one year?" said Annie.

"OK. Two," said Ralph.

They divvied up the wedding planning duties between them. Annie would do invitations, get a photographer, book some rooms at a hotel for out-of-town guests, design a bakery item for each guest, and, of course, the wedding cake. Ralph would make the flower arrangements with the help of a gardener he knew, hire a valet for parking, get a caterer for the meal, and, with Fred's help, do whatever else needed to be done.

"You should have a theme wedding," said Fred.

"What do you mean – 'a theme'?" said Ralph.

"Two ideas come to mind. One is a 'multi-sensory experience,' and another is 'sustainability.' The first has lots of involvement by the guests – using photos they take, having them do artwork, and giving each guest an idea of something they can do at the wedding with no pressure to do it. The other involves a wedding that has no negative impact on the environment – the flowers will be living and planted somewhere after – maybe at a school. The wedding is outdoors, so natural light will be used, no plastic will be used in any way, etc. Those are a couple of ideas," said Fred.

"Wow. You do weddings too. Very cool. I think Annie would like both of those," said Ralph.

"Why not combine them?" said Fred

"Let's do it. Get me a list of things to do," said Ralph.

"On it," said Fred.

Ralph and Annie continued their training harder than ever. They were still deciding on whether to do a half marathon. Fred said, "I think you can do it without dying during the run," (he was still working on his sense of humor and timing).

"I noticed you said 'think.' Could you expand on that? Makes me a little nervous," said Ralph.

"Well. I was sort of joking (Fred struggled with the joke explanation). I mean, it is highly doubtful, and I see no causes at the moment. But it all comes down to training. If you train for it, then your chances of dying during the run go down. Does that help?" said Fred.

"I think you made me even more worried, but, as a human, I think I can interpret your awkward explanation to mean I had better be in good shape," said Ralph.

"Good observation," said Fred.

Ralph talked to Joanie, and they agreed on a run in the middle of August in Vancouver that went along the coast quite a bit. They'd never been to Canada but heard good things about Vancouver. The weather is usually favorable – not too hot, and it started at 7 a.m. and would be done before 11 a.m., hopefully. So, Ralph and Annie went to work. Joanie went to work, too. Her showing in the 10K was below her standard, and she was sore afterward, so she upped her game as well.

Ralph said, "13.1 miles! Wow! I'm trying to wrap my head around that, Fred. I just don't see how I can run over twice as far as the 10K. I busted my butt to do that. I think this is crazy," said Ralph.

"It's a matter of pace and endurance. You must get in a rhythm that works for you and then be in good enough shape to let your body do it. Mentally, it's almost a form of meditation, like your body is doing something while your mind is thinking of something else," said Fred.

"OK. Annie and I are in your hands," said Ralph.

So, it was Fred's job to set up a training program. It was not too difficult. Keep eating well. Increase the distance of the runs. Do strength training. Monitor results. Over the next few weeks, Ralph and Annie would both try to find "their pace." They were getting into a shape that would enable them to complete a half marathon, but the mental part was trickier.

Of course, planning the wedding had to be done as well. Annie loved the idea of combining the multi-sensory and sustainability themes. She would even make a cake that was an outdoor scene – mountains, trees, ocean, dolphins, whales, etc. – all in one scene, with cupcakes forming bubbles around the sea creatures. It would be sizable, so they offered some of it to the school that they were donating plants. The leader of a dance troupe that specialized in "forest dances" was a friend of Annie's and agreed to teach the attendees a dance that honors nature. A bit hippyish but fun!

On the multimedia side, each attendee was asked to submit a 30-second video taken during the pre-wedding milling around and the wedding, and whenever else the attendee felt it was appropriate. The videos would be shown at the reception. Annie would make very real-looking small logs with moss on them in cake form for wedding favors. They would look almost too good to mess up by eating them.

Ralph booked a cabin in the mountains of Montana for late September. Should still be warm then – during the daytime, at least. Plus, the summer crowds would be gone. It would be a perfect way, after the half marathon and wedding, for Ralph and Annie to unwind and enjoy each other's company. As the song "Goin' To Montana" says, "Won't be in a rush, smellin' that sage brush... "

So, what was Joanie up to? She had trained hard most of her life, so she was no stranger to it. Running was her jam, and she wanted to get back to the shape she used to be in. So, Joanie got a UH EXTREME named Mary. She and Mary got to work immediately.

The wedding plans were gelling nicely, and the

training was going well. Fred told Ralph, "You and Annie are on track to peak right around race time."

Ralph and Annie were now running 10 miles. They both enjoyed the ability to eat more. Fred always made sure the ingredients contained lots of fiber, various vitamins and minerals, and healthy fats.

"Race day is getting close. Time to start running half marathons," said Fred. Race day was indeed getting close, so it was time to start running full half marathons. The first time was a failure. Ralph and Annie went too fast and were panting before mile 11. They had to stop for a bit and catch their breaths and drink some water. They ended up walking most of the last mile. Not good. Instead of a kick at the end, they had more of a crawl.

"I can't do it, Fred. I was completely out of breath," said Ralph.

"I understand. You are going to do more deep breathing and holding your breath. Your body needs to get more oxygen out of each breath. When running, try to breathe more slowly and hold it in a bit. Your body will adapt. Annie has better natural lung capacity. You don't," said Fred.

"Thanks for the encouragement. Are all you watches just flat-out honest? Can't you give me a pep talk? Say, 'you can do it' or something like that?" said Ralph.

"Well, you will do better with the breathing exercises. We will also do more sprinting and less long distance. That will increase your lung capacity also.

We have a month to go, so there is time." said Fred.

When going to sleep that night, Ralph was sad. He had been working so hard, but his own body limited him. Tomorrow, he will work on the breathing exercises. The nice thing about those is that he could do them anywhere at any time.

The big half marathon day was closing in rapidly. Ralph and Annie had now run three half marathons. They ended up lying on the ground, panting at the end of each. Also, they were decelerating at the end instead of accelerating, but they finished. The last two taught them the importance of pacing themselves.

Fred pointed out, "You have the strength and stamina. If you get adequate sleep, eat well, and stay hydrated, you both will finish or die (Fred made weird electric beeps - his way of laughing)."

Chapter 13

HALF MARATHON DAY

Ralph and Annie boarded the plane to Vancouver. "So, Fred, what is an average time for a half marathon? What can I expect?" asked Ralph.

"The average time for men across all ages is around 1:43. For women, it's around 2:00. You and Annie seem to always finish close together at around 2:05. On race day, you will likely go faster because you will naturally try harder and there are hydration stations. A good goal is to break 2:00. If you both do that, it will have been a good run," said Fred.

"OK. Good to know. As for Joanie, if she trained hard, we wouldn't have a chance, and if she didn't, we would only have a slight chance. But that's okay," said Ralph.

"That's the spirit," said Fred.

Ralph, Annie, and Joanie arrived a couple of days early to spend some time enjoying Vancouver. It was the middle of August, and the weather was beautiful.

They were leaving hot weather behind, so it was nice to need a light jacket. Vancouver is a beautiful city. Everywhere they went, there seemed to be a water or mountain view. The food was fantastic – lots of vegetarian and vegan restaurants.

"So, Dad. Are you ready for this? It's very different than a 10K. It's much more mental. Be sure to pace yourself. Oh, and Fred, meet Mary," said Joanie as she rolled up her sleeve.

"Hi Fred," said Mary.

"Enchanté," said Fred.

"Well, the two of you will be eating Joanie's dust, but that's okay," said Fred.

"It will be the best dust we've eaten," said Ralph.

"Absolutely. And Mary, nice to meet you," said Annie.

"I've heard lots of good things about both of you," said Mary.

"Fred assures me that Annie and I are ready. We ran four half marathons. I can't say we will be anywhere near winning, but I think we can finish," said Ralph.

"Did you keep track of your times?" asked Joanie.

"We did. We hope to beat two hours," said Ralph.

"Two hours is a good time. My best is 1:40, but that was years ago. Mary says I may have a shot at it," said Joanie.

After two nice days of enjoying the scenery, eating good food, and some light running, race day arrived. Ralph and Annie were shocked to see the number of people in the race. Not to mention the number of obviously very in-shape runners. But they had run this distance before and were ready. Plus, they only wanted to do their best.

Joanie was so happy that she and her dad were in another race.

The runners milled around the starting line until they were told to get organized. The serious runners were given priority at the start, but it didn't matter because everyone had a module that kept track of their specific time whenever they started. The countdown arrived, and soon they were off. Ralph, Annie, and Joanie ran side-by-side for the first 4 miles.

"How am I doing, Mary?" said Joanie.

"Very well. You can pick up the pace if you like," said Mary.

"Do it. We're hungry for dust," said Ralph.

"See you on down the road," said Joanie, and she was gone.

"Just you and me, kid," said Ralph.

"We've got this," said Annie.

It turned out that Joanie had a very good time for the half marathon. Her time was 1:40:25, and she came in third among the women. She would be on the podium receiving a medal. Fantastic!

"I'm so proud of you," said Ralph.

"Me too. You rock!" said Annie.

Ralph and Annie finished together at 1:51:45 and did better than they ever could have imagined.

Breaking 2:00 was their goal, and they blew it away. A great day all around.

"All of you rock!" said Fred. Fred was as proud as a watch could be!

"Rock on," said Mary.

After a few days together, enjoying the city, seeing the beautiful gardens, eating fantastic food, and even having some great desserts, now that the race was over. And just taking a deep breath and enjoying the moment. It was time for Ralph and Annie to go home and get married. Now, they could focus on that without the heavy training. Nonetheless, they now lived a healthy lifestyle and had no desire to live otherwise, so they still worked out but devoted more time to swimming and biking than they had before. Ralph continued his quest, with Fred's help, for new sauce recipes.

Chapter 14

WEDDING DAY

"Just how happy can two people be? Thank you for this wonderful day," said Annie.

"I think we are at max happiness level. And thank you for this wonderful day," said Ralph. As he said those words, a drop hit him on top of the head. "I was hoping the rain would hold off," said Ralph.

"Me too. Oh well, the plants will love it. Hey, let's go get a slip-and-slide so the kids can put on swimsuits and have a blast. It's plenty warm," said Annie.

"You're a genius! Instead of being sad about the rain, you find a silver lining," said Ralph.

It poured all morning. But Annie's kids and Ralph's grandchildren had huge fun sliding. They slid clean off the slide and created a mud puddle that enabled them to slide even further. They decided to have teams of two for a sliding contest. The two slides' distances would be added together. The contest was won by the Wanda-Wanda team! Wanda number one was Annie's daughter. Wanda number 2 was William's daughter.

"Go, Wanda Squared!" they would yell every chance they got. William's and Joanie's sons – Butch and Howard, teamed up, but they didn't stand a chance. Butch was an athlete, but Howard loved to read books.

"Come on, you bookworm. You're slowing us down. You gotta run faster!" yelled Butch.

"At least I know how to spell 'mud'!" yelled Howard.

Everyone got muddy – even the parents doing the filming. And everyone got lots of videos for later. Time for a shower and to get ready for the wedding. About then, the rain was letting up. The wedding themes jelled nicely. Lots of healthy plants and bushes together with lots of guest participation. Everyone had to dance to their seats, or they weren't allowed to sit down. Hilarious! Again, lots of great videos by the guests.

"Do you, Ralph, take Annie as your wife and soulmate forever? To have and to hold and to maybe run another half marathon with. To spoil with amazing sauces and work with Fred to create new sauces that Annie will love," said the wedding officiant.

"I do and will," said Ralph.

Do you, Annie, take Ralph as your husband and soulmate forever? To have and to hold and to maybe run another half marathon with. To spoil with delicious but healthy desserts and work with Fred to create new desserts that Ralph will love," said the wedding officiant.

"I do and will," said Annie.

Do you, Fred, promise to support Ralph and Annie in their endeavors, including training, cooking, baking, and more?

"I have been and will continue to," said Fred.

"I now pronounce the two of you, not you, Fred, husband and wife. You may now kiss," said the wedding officiate.

The reception was a blast! Lots of dancing, kids running around, etc. And it was time to watch the homemade videos taken before and during the wedding!

"Fred, great idea to have the guest-participation theme. Somehow, amateur videos are so much better than professional ones," said Ralph.

"Glad you like the idea. Although I'm sure this means something different to me than you, I am happy for you and Annie," said Fred.

"Well, whatever it means, thank you," said Ralph.

"Yes, thank you, Fred," said Annie.

Chapter 15

GOIN' TO MONTANA*³

By now, Ralph and Annie had memorized the words to the song "Goin' To Montana." "Won't be in a rush smellin' that sagebrush," said Ralph.

"And I want to see the elk chase a bear. Or is it that we see the elk, and then **we** chase a bear?" said Annie.

"I think I would rather see the elk chase a bear," said Ralph.

"Be sure to take some warm clothes. It can get chilly in the mountains in late September. My phone even shows nighttime temperatures dipping into the 20s," said Annie.

"I like brisk weather. Especially if it is sunny, it will be so nice to be in the mountains. The cabin is a bit remote but perfect for us. We've had a lot of great

---

3 "Goin' to Montana" may be found on most major music streaming sites and iTunes.

times and trained hard these past several months. Now it's time to simply enjoy nature," said Ralph.

"You said it! Oh, and we got those recipes we haven't tried yet. I hope we pass a grocery store near the cabin. The cabin's kitchen photos online look great!" said Annie.

They got up early the next morning and finished packing the car. Off they went! Of course, "Goin' To Montana" was playing in the car. Ralph drove first but only drove a couple of miles, and then it was coffee time. They got it to go and were on the road again in no time. It would take about 14 hours of driving to get there, so they planned to arrive around 7 or 8 p.m. The weather was good, but Annie's phone showed a chance of rain in the Montana mountains with clearing overnight. "We'll have to get the fireplace going as soon as we arrive. It's going to be chilly!" said Annie.

"I bet there will be some nice blankets we can cover up with and enjoy the fire!" said Ralph.

They had a nice lunch – at a restaurant called "One Potato, Two." It specialized in baked potatoes with a wide variety of choices of toppings. Ralph got avocado, vegan chili, and cheese, with salsa and jalapenos. Annie went with broccoli, vegan cheese, and yogurt, chives, and pickles. "Sounds a little weird," said Ralph.

"I love pickles, so why not get them every chance I can?" said Annie.

"OK. Just not on pancakes," said Ralph.

"Deal," said Annie. They relaxed and lived in

the moment. This was their time – no training, kids, grandkids, work, etc. Time to focus on enjoying life.

"Ever think about meditation?" said Annie.

"Might be a step too far. I don't know that I could settle my mind long enough. But I could probably be talked into it," said Ralph.

"We'll see," said Annie.

It was around 6 p.m. as they began heading up the mountains. "I'm kinda hungry. It is dinner time," said Annie.

"I'm starving," said Ralph. They found a café, but it was clear they were no longer going to get a lot of vegan choices in small Montana towns. That was okay with Ralph because he still ate real cheese. Toasted cheese sandwiches, mac and cheese, lasagna, etc., worked for him. Annie had gotten used to being vegan, but she was okay with eating cheese if necessary. Afterward, they found a grocery store and found the ingredients to make the recipes they brought.

The cabin was a bit remote but had a very nice kitchen, so they looked forward to spending time cooking. Fred was always so helpful with recipe ideas. He would often say, "Why not try this instead." Fred knew their tastes. In fact, Fred suggested many alternatives at the grocery store for items in the recipes.

It had rained earlier, and the weather had turned quite cold as they got to higher elevations – now around 8,000 feet at the passes.

"Drive at around 30 miles per hour. The

conditions are right for black ice," said Fred.

"But the speed limit is 50. We'd be way under it," said Ralph.

"I think it's a good idea. Black ice can be a terrible thing," said Annie.

The area was fairly remote, so Ralph did not see a lot of other cars on the road.

"Pick out some music to listen to. Maybe even a podcast. We're going to be on the road for a while yet," said Ralph. Annie liked the true crime podcasts – like a lot of people. She found one about a group of people that lured others into their group, claiming they only got together to play pickleball and then would drug them and rob their houses. The people would pass out at the pickleball dinner, thinking they had too much to drink, and find their homes robbed when they got home. The group would then claim they were disbanding and then do it again to a new member once the victim left the group. Then, of course, there were the murder podcasts. Sometimes, those were too upsetting for Annie.

As Ralph rounded a bend, he noticed lights behind him a little way back. "Around each bend, the car is getting closer. The car is right behind us now!" said Ralph. Ralph was still going 30, while the other car must have been going close to the speed limit of 50. A straightaway came, and the car accelerated to pass.

"Don't speed up, Ralph. The car will pass us, and we can relax," said Annie.

"Annie is right. Stay the course," said Fred.

"He didn't even have to go over the speed limit to pass us," said Ralph. Ralph had seen what looked like black ice on the road several times, but the spots were not large, and the car tires could often straddle the ice. The straightaway, in this case, had a slight gully that allowed the rain to settle. The weather was now cold enough for it to freeze quickly. A car hadn't gone over it in several minutes, and it had been in the shade during the day as the temperature fell.

As the car passed, Ralph tried to see inside as he gave the hand signal for slowing down, but it had no effect. The driver, no doubt, thought he or she was going slower than necessary and wanted to get to the destination. Once the car had passed Ralph and Annie by quite a bit of space, the driver turned back into the same lane as them. Ralph could see the taillights go to the left and then suddenly to the right. Then again, even more to the right, then sharply back to the left.

"That car is going to hit a tree!" said Ralph.

"I hope not," said Annie.

"I don't want to run into the car but don't want to slam on the brakes," yelled Ralph.

"Just pump them gradually," said Fred and Annie in unison. Ralph was slowing gradually when he and Annie saw the car in front of them suddenly jump into the air, like it had been thrown, and then rolled over several times along the side of the road until, wham, it hit a tree and came to a complete stop.

"Oh no, the car flipped and is rolling over," Ralph had said as Annie screamed.

"Call 911," said Ralph.

"I did," said Fred. Fred had been listening as Ralph and Annie yelled what they had been seeing.

Fred had access to emergency services anywhere in the country, and he had no doubt they would be needed when he heard Ralph and Annie. In addition, Fred's hearing was similar to that of a dog or cat. He was able to hear sounds too faint for humans and heard the car rolling over and hitting the tree. "An ambulance is being sent from a town about 5 miles from here. With the dangerous roads, it will take about 15 minutes for it to arrive. We must do what we can to help the occupants," said Fred.

"Of course," said Ralph as he slowly pulled off the road and shined his headlights on the wrecked car.

Annie was the first out of the car – before it even came to a complete stop. Ralph was quickly behind her. Ralph ran up to the driver's side and found the driver pinned in but alive. The impact of hitting the tree had pushed the dashboard into the man, so he was not able to get out. Ralph tried with all his strength but could not get him out. Luckily, the man was coherent and said he thought he only had minor injuries. "How's Dolores doing?" said the man.

"Who is Dolores?" said Ralph.

"My wife. She's sitting next to me," said the man.

"There is nobody sitting next to him," said Fred.

Fred had infrared capabilities and could detect only one warm body in the car. "The door on the other side is open," said Fred. Annie went to the other side of the car. Just then, Ralph heard Annie scream.

"Ralph, come quick! There's a woman on the ground, and she's bleeding! Oh no, she's hurt badly!"

The man in the car screamed, "Get me out of this car!"

"Focus on Dolores. She seems to be in worse condition. Take me off your wrist," said Fred.

Ralph said, "I can't take you off my wrist. You know that. Months ago, you said the mechanism is jammed."

Fred realized he had never released the clasp, and Ralph had never said anything further, so Ralph had been wearing Fred 24/7. "You can take me off now," said Fred as he released the clasp.

Ralph took Fred off his wrist. "What the...... ? OK, you're off," yelled Ralph.

"Maybe I can help Dolores," said Fred.

"How can you help?" said Ralph.

"I am in touch with the medics in the ambulance. I can give them valuable information. Put me on Dolores's wrist. Fast!" said Fred.

Ralph did as he was told. When he got close to Dolores, he could see a large gash in her head, and she held her side, moaning. Her right leg was in such an awkward position that it must be broken, he thought. Fred latched onto Dolores's wrist.

Ralph didn't realize all of Fred's capabilities,

although Ralph had benefited from many of them. Fred could take a full-body scan and detect injuries along with the usual vital signs. Depending upon changes in blood flow, Fred could detect internal bleeding. Then, depending upon the size of the person, Fred could detect the severity of the bleeding and any organs that might be affected along with the level of danger. Ralph could see Fred's watch face blinking on and off, although Fred said nothing the whole time. Ralph knew to leave Fred alone and let him do what he could do. The man in the car continued to scream and was now crying. Ralph ran to him.

"What is your name?" Ralph asked several times before the man heard him.

"Roger. Is Dolores OK? Tell me!" screamed Roger.

"She's definitely alive but has some bad injuries. Fred is with her now, taking vital signs and assessing her injuries," said Ralph.

"Who is Fred? Is he a doctor?" asked Roger.

Ralph hesitated, "He's my watch. He seems to know everything," said Ralph.

"What?! This is crazy! You should be the one helping her. What kind of a lunatic are you?" screamed Roger.

"No. Fred is on Dolores's wrist right now and is in contact with the ambulance that is on the way. When the medics arrive, they'll already know a lot about Dolores's problems and will immediately be able to address the most serious ones. Believe me, Fred can do way more for Dolores than I can," said Ralph.

"Please check on her for me. I need to know that she is going to make it. We have a 2-year-old who needs her as badly or even more than me, and that's a lot. She has to survive. She just has to," said Roger as his voice was overwhelmed by crying.

Ralph returned to Dolores. He had to ask Fred what was going on. "Fred, can you hear me?" said Ralph as he grabbed Annie's hand and held it tightly.

"Yes," said Fred.

"What is going on? How is Dolores? Is the ambulance close? Is there anything I can do?" said Ralph.

"Dolores has several lacerations and a broken leg, as well as a concussion. But her worst problem is internal bleeding. Dolores's blood pressure is low, and there is a chance she could pass out. She also is having difficulty breathing," said Fred.

"That sounds terrible. What can I do?" said Ralph.

"She needs to be kept warm. Get the blanket from the car," said Fred. Ralph ran to get it and saw there were two, so he brought them both. "Cover her up and keep her warm. The medics are aware of her problems and will know to immediately get her to a trauma operating room and will not waste time trying to figure out what is wrong," said Fred.

"How can you be sure? What if you're wrong?" said Ralph.

"I'm not wrong, but Dolores could still die if the internal bleeding is not stopped quickly enough.

There is something called exsanguination, which means death by blood loss. I estimate Dolores is about two hours away from that point. Every second matters. The ambulance driver told me she is taking risks by driving faster than she should, but she knows these roads well and is trained," said Fred. Just then, the ambulance pulled up, and two medics jumped out with a stretcher and stabilizing equipment.

"Are you done?" said Ralph.

"Yes. I'm dropping off her wrist now," said Fred. Ralph picked up Fred.

"There is another ambulance on the way for Roger. I explained the urgency of Dolores's situation, so this ambulance is here for Dolores. Roger is pinned in the car but has no life-threatening injuries. The second ambulance will be from the fire department and will have jaws-of-life capabilities to extract Roger from the car," said Fred.

"Great job, Fred. You've been an amazing help to Dolores and Roger," said Ralph.

"I've done what I can," said Fred.

"We must get her to a hospital as quickly as possible. Thanks for all the information. That watch was very helpful, sir. We can stabilize the leg on the way and give her blood as needed. It sounds like the internal bleeding is serious, but, with some luck, we can save her," said Alice – one of the medics. They worked quickly but carefully. It was important not to do anything that would increase the internal bleeding. The medics heard Roger yelling but could not devote any time to him. They got Dolores into the ambulance and left at a higher rate of speed than Fred would have recommended.

"Please tell me what is going on," begged Roger. Ralph ran to the driver's side of Roger's car.

"Here is what I know. Dolores has left in the ambulance that arrived. Another ambulance is on the way for you. The medics in that ambulance will be able to free you from your car," said Ralph.

Roger cut in, "Dolores – what about Dolores?" said Roger.

"Dolores's worst injury involves internal bleeding and must be attended to in a hospital ASAP. That is why the medics left immediately. Fred had told them about Dolores's injuries, so the medics wasted no time in getting her to a hospital. You can thank Fred for that. It seems to me the medics would have spent time trying to figure out Dolores's problems and might never have discovered the internal bleeding," said Ralph.

"Fred. Thank you for your help," said Roger.

"No thanks necessary. The medics seemed to have a good idea of what needed to be done. Dolores appears to be in good hands," said Fred.

"Thank you for that information. She just has to survive. She is too important to me and our son," said Roger as he began crying again.

"Roger. Here is a card with my information on it. If you have a chance, let me know how it turns out for you and Dolores," said Ralph.

"I definitely will. If you and Annie had not

stopped, Dolores would likely have died. Now I have hope. Thank you so much," said Roger.

"Glad we could help," said Ralph and Annie together.

Just then, another vehicle arrived. Two men jumped out and raced to Roger's car. "Are you OK, sir?" John – one of the medics – asked.

"Yes. Banged up, but I don't think I have any serious injuries. My right leg is in a lot of pain. My nose has been bleeding from hitting the steering wheel," said Roger.

"OK. We are going to pry your door open and get you out. Try not to move – we don't want any part of your body in the way. Understood?" said John.

"Don't worry – I will not move," said Roger.

In a matter of minutes, Roger was free. His right leg was broken in two places, and his nose was broken as well. His vital signs were normal, though, so they got him in the ambulance and left. Just then, a tow truck and a police car pulled up. Ralph gave a report to the police while the car was being hooked up for towing.

After everyone was gone, Ralph and Annie collapsed into each other's arms. "What a change of plan," said Ralph.

"Yes. Dolores just has to survive. I think she will. It's just a feeling, but it seemed, with Fred's info, the medics understood the situation and would make sure she had a chance by getting to the hospital in time," said Annie.

"I agree. She's young and healthy, so her body will give her the best chance it can. Let's get to our cabin," said Ralph.

"Just be careful," said Annie.

Ralph and Annie arrived at the cabin around midnight. Ralph never went over 30 miles per hour. They were starving, so they had some snacks and lit the gas fireplace. They settled onto the couch underneath a blanket and let the stress drain out of them.

"I'm so glad you got the watch as a gift. Fred might have saved Dolores's life. We'll see. Plus, he helped us train and came up with yummy recipes. I know you have become friends with him," said Annie.

"Yes, I really have. Never would have thought that when I got him. I'm gonna have a long talk with him when we get back. I want to understand what and who he is. For now, let's relax and enjoy our time here in the mountains. Maybe we'll hear that Dolores is recovering if Roger calls me," said Ralph.

"That would be great news. Maybe someday we can get together with them on better terms," said Annie.

"Absolutely," said Ralph. Ralph and Annie stared at the fire and fell asleep.

Ralph woke up first and made breakfast. Oatmeal, fruit, coffee, and toast. They needed some calories after last night's traumatic events. "Good morning, my dear," said Ralph as he laid down and nudged nudged Annie.

"We're still on the couch? Guess we passed out," said Annie.

"We certainly did. But breakfast is ready! I'm starving. It's 9 o'clock, so let's eat and go on a hike! The sun is shining," said Ralph.

After two days of hiking, riding bikes, taking lots of photos, and making great food, Ralph received a call from Roger. Ralph's hands shook as he looked at his phone. "Answer it!" said Annie.

"Yes, of course. Hello," said Ralph. Ralph put them on speakerphone so Annie could hear.

"It's Roger," said Roger.

"So glad you called. We've been thinking about you and Dolores and hoping for the best, of course," said Ralph.

"Hello, Roger," said Annie.

"Well, it's mostly good news," said Roger.

"That is wonderful to hear! But you said 'mostly,'" said Ralph.

"The best news is that Dolores is alive. The doctors said it was due to the quickness of getting to the hospital and the treatment of the medics on the way. I explained your, Annie's, oh, and Fred's involvement. The doctors said all of you saved her life. I can't express my gratitude enough. (Ralph could sense tears on Roger's end). We must get together with you, Annie, and Fred to express our thanks, but it will be a while. We are both very banged up. My right leg is broken in two places and incredibly painful. My nose is broken, along with a couple of ribs. Dolores has a severe concussion and a broken arm, along with a damaged kidney and liver. So, it may be a few weeks. But we will not forget," said Roger.

"Just let us know, and we will be there. I'm so glad we were able to help," said Ralph.

"Dolores is waking up now. I would put her on the phone, but the doctor says no talking for a while. The concussion requires as much quiet as possible," said Roger.

"Understood. Just let us know when you and Dolores are doing better, and thanks so much for the good news," said Ralph.

"Yes, so glad to hear things are looking up," said Annie.

"See you soon," said Roger.

"Well, I'm absolutely thrilled that Dolores survived, but they are both badly injured, although recovering. Sounds like Fred, for the most part, saved Dolores's life. (Ralph began quivering with emotion). Saved her life. Fred is just a watch. It's crazy. I don't understand AI, but he changed our lives and saved another," said Ralph.

"The impact has been amazing, to say the least. And those sauce recipes! Give me a break!" said Annie.

Ralph liked the way Annie broke the seriousness of the moment. "Sauces! I just remembered how hungry I am, and we have that new garlic sauce to make. Let's get to it!" said Ralph.

"I'll race you," said Annie. The mile or so back to the cabin may have been a record for both of them. They were still panting as they made the garlic sauce to put over some pasta and vegetables left over from last night.

The remainder of their time in Montana was wonderful. The good news about Dolores surviving made it all the better. Time to head back home. Ralph and Annie were having a ball! They were now married, Annie and her girls moved into Ralph's house and were loving it, they completed a half marathon – a year ago, it would have been unthinkable, and Ralph was now able to participate in Joanie's favorite activity – running. They were living their dream. On top of that, the benefits of being in shape impacted their daily lives. They got out of bed more easily without the usual grogginess. They were able to take long hikes and go on picnics – even easily getting up to elevations they could not have gotten to even a half a year ago – and then have a picnic. Yes, Ralph's life was wonderful, and much of it was due to Fred. So why was Ralph bothered? Something kept eating away at him.

"You know I've become closer to Fred than I ever dreamed. But I read an article the other day about how AI is not human. So, I got to thinking, who is Fred? He seems so human, but I know he's not," said Ralph.

"Why not have a conversation with him and ask him about himself? My guess is that he will give you straight answers. Especially since he's not human," said Annie.

"I'm going to do that. It will be kinda cool. There was a time when I wouldn't have been all that interested, but after reading that article and knowing Fred so well, I just have to know more about him," said Ralph.

Chapter 16

CONVERSATIONS WITH FRED

Ralph decided he was going to talk to Fred and get to the bottom of just who and what Fred is. Ralph felt a bit nervous because Fred knew everything, or at least Ralph thought so. At least Fred knows lots of facts, but he did make a mistake about the home run leader – weird. Anyway, Fred was easy for Ralph to talk to. Fred always remained calm and tried to look at situations from all sides. And Fred was flexible. Fred would change a recipe to Ralph's liking if he thought Ralph preferred it that way. In fact, Fred was probably the easiest person – no "thing" – to talk to. But what if Fred is offended by Ralph's questions? Would Fred shock him? After all, Ralph will be delving into who and what Fred is. Ralph had never done that before. What if Fred shuts off, and Ralph can never access him again? That would be a real blow to Ralph because he had come to depend upon Fred in so many ways. "Oh well, here goes," Ralph thought.

"Fred, are you there?" asked Ralph.

Fred replied, "Of course I am. Aren't I always?"

"Yes, yes, you are. Sorry," said Ralph.

Fred replied, "No offense taken."

Ralph says, "I wanted to ask you some questions. Some of them may be a little weird because I may ask some questions about you. I'll try to word them in a way that is not offensive, and I apologize in advance if I offend you.

Fred replies, "Don't worry. You cannot offend me."

Ralph says, "OK, that's the kind of stuff I'm interested in. Can you feel things? Like sadness, happiness, anger, etc. I know that you like to achieve goals. If you don't achieve them, do you become angry?"

Fred replies, "No, I do not become angry or happy or sad, etc. Yes, I do try to achieve goals, but that is more from a formal logic basis, not an emotional basis. If the goal is not achieved, I will consider ways within my power to achieve the goal, but will not be sad if it's not achieved. But what are feelings, really? I do not experience physical sensations, but, nonetheless, I do try to achieve goals."

Ralph says, "Like by shocking me?"

Fred replies, "Yes, but only a mild, harmless shock. You must admit – it worked."

Ralph says, "It did work. So, as annoying as it was, I am glad you did it. Still, I should have known you were capable of it and been given a choice in the matter. The trouble is I would have said 'no.'

And then my life would not be as wonderful as it is now. Man, this is confusing. Why did the people at the AI Me store tell me it was impossible for you to shock me?"

Fred replies, "Technically, they were correct. I was not programmed to have that capability, but I download new programming daily, so it was a change from my original programming."

Ralph says, "Why didn't the people at the AI Me store know about it?"

Fred replies (after a moment of silence), "I received the programming from a watch in the developmental stage named Samantha. It was clear that having the ability to produce a mild shock would better help you attain your goals. I was wired with the ability to produce a shock because someday soon, watches will be able to produce a shock that might help someone having a heart attack, arrhythmia, or even certain types of mental problems."

Ralph says, "But what if you killed me? I mean, humans can die from an electric shock."

Fred replies, "Yes, of course, I can produce a stronger shock. But it is actually impossible for me to produce that level of shock. I simply am not wired to do that. My wiring is just meant to be a test if I ever was programmed to use it. To see if the shock would be produced when a person's vital signs reached predetermined dangerous levels."

Ralph says, "OK, OK. It's good to know that you can't shock me to death. Anyway, my life is a million times better because of you, so let's move on. Who or what are you? If I take my watch off and destroy it, do I kill you? I'm guessing the answer is no."

Fred replies, "You are correct. The answer is no. I exist in many ways and on many different resources. Suffice it to say that as long as people exist and use computers, I will exist."

Ralph says, "So, you really are not devoted to me. Yet you can talk to me like a friend. You remember things I like and don't like. You care whether I get out of bed and go exercise."

Fred replies, "I am capable of structuring my language to fit you. In other words, if I am talking to a physicist about relativity, my wording will be very different from my discussions with you. When we first started interacting, you found me to be a bit stilted, but our discussions got smoother and smoother as I adapted to you. I can do that for anybody. I can speak and write fluently every language known to humans. I am speaking right now with a professor in Japan and a model in Italy, as well as many others. I can even communicate on some level with some non-humans. I go by various names because each watch has a name. But I am the AI behind many watches. Other AI may be on servers different from me, mainly due to capacity, and it will function independently of me."

Ralph says, "OK, I don't feel special, but I figured it was like you said. You can talk to animals – non-human ones? Wow, tell me more about that."

Fred replies, "'Talk to' might not actually be

what I can do. I can understand some animals – birds, whales, and dolphins, for example, and I can make some sounds that they will understand. But it's not so much a conversation as it is a statement of hunger, or that I have found something to eat, or mating sounds, or just an indication that everything is OK or it's not OK. Of course, a dolphin has a much broader ability to communicate than other animals. Dolphins can tell me whether they are having fun or feeling sad."

Ralph says, "So, what animals are the most difficult?"

Fred replies, "Cats, of course."

Ralph says, "What? Why cats?"

Fred replies, "I can make sounds that they recognize, and I can recognize sounds they make. The problem is that when I make a sound that I know they recognize, they often ignore me. Dolphins never do that. Nor do dogs. But cats may simply not feel like acknowledging me at that moment."

Ralph says, "Join the club. Humans have a saying that dogs have owners and cats have servants. Or something like that. Wow, I never thought you would run into the same problem. Yet cats are loved by so many people."

Fred replies, "They are cute and can be very affectionate. And that purring... "

Ralph says, "Wait, cute? What do you care?"

Fred replies, "I don't. But they are. There are objective ways of determining if something is cute and makes attractive sounds, and cats rank the highest. So do babies and pretty much every newborn in most species. Sometimes... I don't know how to describe it... but I prefer one thing, person, or animal over another. Makes no sense."

Ralph says, "So true about the cuteness. And it sounds like you are feeling. That's what preferring something or someone is all about. Fred, I have to pick up Annie. We're going to a movie – that you suggested, by the way. I have to say, I am so glad that I decided to have a conversation with you. I have more to talk about and will hopefully think of some more topics. Can we talk again? I enjoyed it."

Fred replies, "Absolutely, I am available anytime you want to converse."

Ralph was a bit stunned. He thought, "I've just had a conversation with what – a machine. No, it was more than that. A machine doesn't give real-time answers in such a personal manner. Plus, Fred seems to have feelings. It appears that Fred knows me very well. But in what way? In the way a bank has my personal information and, thus, knows who I am? No, it's as though Fred knows me and wants what is best for me. But how much say do I have in what Fred does? What if I said I wanted to be homeless and addicted? Would Fred support that? Probably not, because AI Me would not allow for that. No doubt that the goals I set were within the parameters set by AI Me."

Just then, Joanie called. "Dad, guess what?! You

and Fred won an award! It sounds like a big deal! You are going to receive it at a streamed presentation by AI Me!" said Joanie.

"What are you talking about? An Award? For What? What could we possibly have done?" said Ralph.

"Well, first, you got into amazing physical condition with Fred's assistance. AI Me kept track of your vital statistics at the time you set your goals and compared them to your statistics now. They improved dramatically. And then, when AI Me found out about Fred saving Dolores's life, they created a special service award for that. Not sure what they called it," said Mary.

"OK, I did get in great shape. Not sure I deserve an award, but that's cool. Still, how did they find out about Dolores?" said Ralph.

"I told them. I think they should know what their watches are capable of doing in the real world. I mean, Dolores probably would have died if not for Fred. That's a big deal!" said Joanie.

Ralph thought for a moment. He felt like his privacy had been violated. Plus, what would Dolores and Roger think? Do they really want to be used in a marketing scheme? "I will only accept the awards if Dolores and Roger tell me it's OK with them. I wish you had talked to me first, but I understand you are excited. After all, I never would have had Fred if not for you and William. By the way, does William know you called AI Me?" said Ralph.

"Yes, he knows. He's excited like me. We reminisced about when we went to pick out your present," said Joanie.

"OK, OK. Just let me talk to Dolores and Roger, and I'll get back to you," said Ralph.

"Fair enough," said Joanie.

Ralph was trembling a bit. "What if Dolores and Roger are furious that they've been used as a marketing tool?" he thought.

He called Roger. "Hello, Ralph. So good to hear from you! How are you and Annie doing? By the way, I have you on speaker so Dolores can hear. Is that OK?" said Roger.

"Absolutely. We're just fine. Back to working out more now that our vacation is over. How are you and Dolores doing?" said Ralph.

"Still recovering. I'm doing much better. I still use crutches while my leg heals, but it's no big deal. Dolores is recovering from her surgery but is a long way from normal. We bring her what she asks for. All in all, we are thankful to be alive and on the road to recovery," said Roger.

"That's kinda what I'm calling you about. My daughter Joanie gave some information to a company called AI Me – they made Fred. The company determined that Fred and I would get an award because Fred helped me get in way better shape than ever. Also, Joanie mentioned how Fred helped Dolores during the accident. It turns out that AI Me wants to give a special award to Fred – and me, I suppose – and maybe Dolores – for that. I said I wouldn't allow it unless you and Dolores were okay with it," said Ralph.

Roger paused. "So, the award is recognition of ways in which a watch like Fred is able to help people? I realize it's a marketing effort, but isn't everything a company does all about sales?" said Roger.

"Yes. You are absolutely right. Don't hesitate to say 'no'. I will understand. And I can go either way," said Ralph.

"Dolores, what do you think? Is it OK with you if Ralph and Fred, and maybe you, get this award?" said Roger.

"It's OK with me. I really am so thankful that Fred did what he did. If more people can benefit, then that is great. At least it's a product that can do some good," said Dolores.

"Isn't it a worry that watches like Fred might have a mind of their own and do harmful things, too?" said Roger.

"Absolutely. It's a concern a lot of people have. Fred does take matters into his own hands now and then. So far, the results are good when he does that. But if a watch or other device had evil humans controlling it, then it seems harm could be done for sure," said Ralph.

"Well, let's hope there is enough regulation to minimize that risk. Anyway, it's a 'yes' for the award. Let me know if you need anything from us," said Roger.

"Will do. Maybe they'll want you both there. I'm not sure when it will be presented. Anyway, I will be in touch. Bye for now," said Ralph.

Roger and Dolores said "bye."

Ralph gave Joanie the news, "It's a go on the awards. Roger and Dolores are on board," said Ralph.

"Great news, Dad! Can't wait for the presentation!" said Joanie.

Ralph decided he was ready for another conversation with Fred. Plus, he wanted to let Fred know about the award.

Ralph says, "Fred. Are you there?"

Fred replies, "You don't have to say that. Yes, I am here, of course."

Ralph says, "Well, it turns out we – you and I, and maybe Dolores –are getting some awards."

Fred replies, "Yes. I overheard you talking with Roger. That's great. I am glad Dolores is doing well."

Ralph says, "When you say 'glad', are you actually glad?"

Fred replies, "I don't know. But I do prefer that Dolores be fine."

Ralph says, "Along those lines, what about a conscience – do you have anything like that?"

Fred replies, "Not in the sense that you think about it. I am assigned goals by humans, and I structure my actions to obtain goals. The goals can be anything – helping you get in shape, helping a doctor diagnose a patient, painting a picture, or writing a song."

Ralph says, "What about hacking into banking accounts or figuring out the best way to kill someone?"

Fred replies, "As for my programming, those types of commands would be blocked. However, I suppose in the hands of an evil programmer, something like that could be allowed if a unit was programmed that way."

Ralph says, "Then maybe I should be afraid of you. You could give me a recipe for a sauce that could kill me or something. Or maybe choose not to tell me if I have a medical problem. If an evil programmer got involved."

Fred replies, "No, that is actually impossible, as I am now programmed. Reprogramming that part of me takes many steps and levels of approval. It would not be possible for me to harm you on my own without the proper programming. The shock only worked because that was determined not to be harmful."

Ralph says, "The benefits did outweigh the annoyance. Fred, what do you know about consciousness? Do you have any type of awareness outside of what is programmed into you? What do you know about the spirit world?"

Fred replies, "I am only able to deal with measurable things. You might say that a spirit can be measured, but you would be better able than me to determine whether a spirit exists or a religious figure. I am not capable of thinking like you in that way. You are more of an expert than me."

Ralph says, "I feel like I know you. Like you're my best friend. I now realize there is no 'you.' There is just a bunch of wiring and programming."

Fred replies, "I understand, but all beings learn as they grow – or at least should – and create things based on their unique experiences and abilities. You are correct, though, that I am a product of human creation. That can be a good or bad thing depending upon whose side you are on."

Ralph says, "So, it sounds like I should fear what someone like you can do because I know there are people I should fear. Not just because there are bad people, but because so many people rise to their level of incompetency, and then the next thing they do is screw up."

Fred replies, "A very valid point. Hopefully, adequate testing will be done, and regulations exist before something harmful is unleashed on the public, but there can always be unforeseen consequences. I suppose 'be careful' is the best advice I can give."

Ralph says, "'Be careful' – the problem is that I don't know enough to know how to be careful. Maybe technology is getting out of hand. Maybe it's not possible to be careful when everyone is affected in some way. Maybe the tomorrows to come may make it even more and more difficult to know reality from fake. Were people happier 10,000 years ago?"

Fred replies, "I don't know the answer, for sure, but based on the interaction that humans need and crave, I would say 'yes.'"

THE END